The Dreamer

L. D. PIERCE

AN AVON FLARE BOOK

THE DREAMER is an original publication of Avon Books. This work has never before appeared in book form.

AVON BOOKS
A division of
The Hearst Corporation
1350 Avenue of the Americas
New York, New York 10019

Copyright © 1996 by Linda Piazza
Published by arrangement with the author
Library of Congress Catalog Card Number: 95-94735
ISBN: 0-380-78062-3
RL: 6.8

First Avon Flare Printing: February 1996

AVON FLARE TRADEMARK REG. U.S. PAT. OFF. AND IN OTHER COUNTRIES, MARCA REGISTRADA, HECHO EN U.S.A.

Printed in the U.S.A.

RA   10 9 8 7 6 5 4 3 2

ONE

Sixteen-year-old Ashley Morgan turned over in bed. Strands of blond hair fell across her face. Half asleep, she brushed them away, then pushed the top sheet down from her arms and shoulders. The room seemed hot, stifling. After a few minutes, she settled into a restless sleep. Soon she was dreaming.

Droplets of sweat stood out against his smooth, mahogany skin as he lay waiting on the floor of the mud-walled room. Pain gnawed at his stomach, but he gritted his teeth and held back the screams. With each breath, his chest rattled, but he did not allow himself to groan.

Rising toward consciousness again, Ashley put her hands to her chest. Her pulse was fast and her breathing too shallow, but before she came fully awake, her breathing deepened and again she slept.

He had watched the members of his village die one by one. His father, the greatest leader of his people, had been one of the first. Now the fever-that-makes-one-bleed had finally struck him, the last male descendant. He turned glassy, red-rimmed eyes toward the door, waiting for the one whom he had summoned with promises of much wealth. He was young and strong, but he could not hold out much

1

longer. Then he heard footsteps approaching the door.

Waking suddenly, Ashley sat up in bed with her eyes wide and her fingers digging into the covers. Her chest hurt, as if she were the one who had been struggling to draw each breath.

Moonlight streamed through the window across from the bed, casting a blue sheen on the cream-colored bedcoverings. Without looking at the clock, Ashley knew that it was far too early to rise. Still, if she stayed in bed a moment longer, the young man's pain and fear would overwhelm her. She kicked off the top sheet. Jumping out of bed, she went over to the floor-to-ceiling bay window, then rested her forehead against the glass. Letting her eyes close, she felt the tears that had gathered beneath her lids.

Turning her head, she glanced at the vincas that her boyfriend, Lucas, had potted for her a few days earlier. The young man in the dream wasn't Lucas. He wasn't anyone that she knew. She didn't know why she dreamed of someone that she didn't know, someone from another time.

Sighing, she looked out at the wooded property that sloped down to the creek. With one hand braced against the window frame, she leaned as far forward as the glass would allow, narrowing her eyes as she studied the landscape. Through breaks in the thick growth of cypresses, pines, and oaks, she could make out the glimmer of moonlight reflected from the water in the creek.

The atmosphere of fear that saturated her dreams had spilled over into her waking life. For weeks now, she had felt some unnamed menace out there.

For all of those weeks, she had repeated this ritual

2

of waking from dreams she barely remembered, then getting up to survey as much of their property as she could see. Sometimes she walked through other rooms, checking windows and doors to make sure that they were locked.

Before turning away, Ashley scanned the line of trees that marked the division between lawn and woods one last time. There was no breeze, but as she watched, it seemed to her that something moved. A shadow wavered and then reformed a few feet back from the edge of the woods.

Moving slowly, she backed away from the window, stopping only when she felt the touch of her footboard across the backs of her legs. She pressed her hands to her abdomen. The pit of her stomach went cold with dread.

It was beginning.

Ashley wasn't a person who usually gave in to premonitions, but the preceding weeks of fear and anxiety had prepared her to expect this moment. There was something to fear out there, and it was coming closer.

Pushing away from the footboard, she crossed her room, then paused in front of the well of darkness that marked the door to the dressing room. She was hesitant to plunge into that darkness, but even more hesitant to turn on the light. If someone really were out there on the edge of the woods, then he would notice when the light came on. He would be able to see into the house.

With her hands sweeping the air in front of her, Ashley made her way through her dressing room, into the bathroom, through a second dressing room, and then out into the connecting room.

One of the two windows in this room faced the

same direction as Ashley's, but here the moonlight picked out the turnings on the legs and rails of an empty crib. Ashley glanced from the crib to the hand-woven rug on the floor, to the changing table, to the array of stuffed animals lining the shelf above the table. All was in readiness for the birth of her younger sister. She and her parents and their house-keeper, Vernettie Blackshear, had prepared the nurs-ery together. Vernettie had begun hooking the rug the moment Ashley's mother had unexpectedly an-nounced her pregnancy.

Lately Ashley had begun to sense that the four of them weren't the only ones waiting for the birth.

Her gaze was drawn back to the stuffed animals. The darkness masked the shaping of their features, the softness of their furred faces. Only their eyes and the buttons on their muzzles caught the moonlight. Their eyes glittered in the reflected light of the moon.

Something slid along the carpet in the hallway. Ashley heard the *woosh, woosh* sound of someone walking barefoot across the carpet.

Holding her breath, she dug her fingernails into her palms. The steps were coming closer.

Woosh, woosh.

"Ashley?" her mother said from the doorway. She snapped on the light.

For a moment, Ashley stood blinking in the sudden light, unable to open her eyes fully. When she could see again, the nursery had returned to its daytime innocence. Stenciled yellow ducks marched in a row around the walls of the room. Folded sheets waited on the new mattress.

"Another bad dream?" her mother asked.

Ashley took in a deep breath, nodding. "Sorry if I woke you," she said.

4

"You didn't. I was already awake." Her mother's nightgown billowed over her round abdomen and then fell in a straight line to the floor. Luxuriant red-gold curls, so different from Ashley's straight, silvery-blond hair, framed her mother's face. Her mother's skin glowed with health. The further her pregnancy progressed, the younger she looked. There was no reason for Ashley to worry about her mother's health, or the baby's, but the unexplained fear had grown as the nightmares came with increasing frequency.

"Have you got any more of that room deodorant you used to spray around to get rid of the bad dreams when I was little?" Ashley asked.

Her mother laughed. "You knew that it was just room deodorant?"

"Yes, but I didn't want to let on. You were trying so hard to help." Ashley laughed, too, only the sound was tight, false.

Her mother didn't seem to be listening any longer. Leaning against the door facing, she traced the outline of her abdomen with her fingertips, gazing with half-closed eyes at the framed print on the wall. It pictured a young girl in a striped pinafore reading to a cat and an assortment of stuffed animals. Ashley looked at the print and then at the animals on the shelf, and a fierce protectiveness for a sister not yet born swept through her. "I don't ever want anything bad to happen to Nikki," she said.

Her mother's eyebrows went up, but still her fingertips moved lightly across her abdomen. "Nikki? You still like the name Nicole best?" Sighing, she straightened, dropping her hands to her side. "Well, we'd better decide," she said, starting out of the room. Glancing over her shoulder at Ashley, she said,

"That's the fourth contraction I've had in twenty minutes. It looks as if your little sister's going to be born today."

The news struck Ashley like a blow to the back of her knees. She reached for the railing of the crib, gripping it in order to hide the sudden trembling of her hands. "Relax," her mother said, laughing. Her laughter drifted back to Ashley as she walked away.

"Oh, no," Ashley whispered. "Oh, no." Today her sister would be born. And, if all went well in the hospital, tomorrow they would bring Nikki home to this nursery.

Ashley looked at the window. Tomorrow night, there would be lights in this nursery. And whoever it was that waited out there would see that Nikki was home.

Early the next evening, Ashley was back in the nursery, looking down at the small, red creature who lay in the crib. A wide expanse of mattress surrounded the infant. "It's impossible that a human being could be that small," Ashley whispered to her father, who stood beside her.

"She weighs more than you did when you were born," he said. "Almost a pound more." His fair hair fell over his forehead as he bent forward to stroke the baby's cheek.

"Impossible," Ashley repeated.

Her father stretched his arms above his head and yawned loudly. At the sound, the baby jumped, her fingers spreading wide and then gathering the sheet as she gripped it.

"You're scaring her!"

Smiling, her father said, "It's just a startle reflex.

All babies do that. Let's go downstairs, big sister, and get something to eat."

"You go ahead," Ashley said. "I'm not hungry yet." She glanced at the window and then back to the baby who lay sleeping with her legs drawn up under her.

As her father left the room, she asked, "Should you wake Mom and ask her if she wants something, too? She might be hungry. She didn't eat much for lunch at the hospital."

"No, it would probably be better to let her sleep for a while."

When her father had gone, Ashley slipped her finger beneath the palm of her little sister. "Nikki," she whispered, as the baby gripped her finger. "You're such a beautiful baby."

It wasn't true. At least, not yet. Nikki's features were tiny and scrunched together, but there was a promise of more beauty to come. Her lower lip was full and tender and her hair a strawberry blond that would probably deepen into a red-gold like their mother's.

From downstairs, Ashley heard the sound of the doorbell ringing. She looked up, listening. The faint sounds of her father's footsteps crossing the marble foyer carried up to her, then the sound of the door opening. After that, Ashley heard another male voice, one that she recognized.

Releasing her finger from her sister's grip, she left the room and walked down the grey-carpeted hall to the top of the stairs. "Lucas," she said. "Come up and see her."

As Lucas climbed toward Ashley, she noticed how thickly his dark-brown hair grew from his scalp. With each step, his khaki slacks pulled tight across

7

muscular thighs. A thin, vertical scar cut across the arch of his eyebrow, giving him a perpetually amused look that she loved. Tonight he looked even more pleased than usual.

"What are you smiling at?" she asked as he climbed the last stair and stood in front of her. Although muscular and athletic, Lucas was only a little above average height. When she stood next to him, or when they sat next to each other at the movies or in the car, her head rested easily on his shoulder.

"This," he said, taking four roses from behind his back.

Ashley grinned. "Did you steal those from your mother's garden?" she asked.

"Of course not," Lucas said, leaning forward and kissing her forehead. "She gave them to me willingly. Rosamar helped me choose the best ones. It's all legal and aboveboard."

"Are they for my mother?" she asked, as she took Lucas's arm and walked with him toward the nursery.

"This one is." Lucas held up the red rose.

They were at the nursery door. Ashley put her fingers over her lips to motion to Lucas to be quiet, then led him forward. He leaned over the crib and looked down at Nikki for a long moment. "Nicole Emilia Morgan, I present you with your first rose," he whispered, placing a delicate, pink bud in the corner of her crib. He placed the red rose for Ashley's mother in the opposite corner.

Ashley smiled with pleasure, glancing up at Lucas. Her gaze lingered on his mouth and his long, straight nose. As she looked at him, she remembered the face of the suffering young man in her dream. It had been a more exotic and mysterious face than Lucas's, but not a more handsome one, she decided.

8

She signaled to him and preceded him out of the nursery. She had known Lucas most of her life. His younger sister, Rosamar, had been Ashley's best friend since the two girls had first started school. Two months earlier, Ashley and Lucas had begun dating while Lucas was home from college on his spring break, and then had continued dating when he returned just last week for the summer. His strength, his kindness, and his gentle humor were the traits that had attracted her to him, but she couldn't help wishing that he might be a little more mysterious. A little more like the young man in her dreams.

Lucas held up the last two roses. They were a deeper pink than the bud that he had placed in the crib. "Oh, I forgot about the other two," she said. "Who are they for?"

Lucas's crooked eyebrow rose. "I thought you might have forgotten what day today is," he said, "but I'll forgive you under the circumstances."

"What day?" Ashley asked. Then she realized the date. It was May 6, two months to the day since their first date. "One rose for each month," she said. She looked up at him. "And we were supposed to go out."

Lucas lifted his arm and looked at his watch. "There's still plenty of time," he said. "I can make reservations while you get dressed."

Ashley leaned forward and kissed his chin. "Ask Dad if he'll find a vase for the flowers," she said. "I'll be down in twenty minutes, tops."

"I'll be waiting," Lucas said.

Maybe it was the reminder in those words that sent the chill down Ashley's back, or maybe it was the thought of leaving her little sister for the first time. She watched Lucas's broad back as he headed

9

for the top of the stairs, and then she turned and looked at the open nursery door. Hurrying into the nursery, she scooped up her little sister. She carried her into the master suite, and put her down beside her sleeping mother in the king-size bed. She piled the extra pillows around the baby, then tiptoed to the door.

When she looked back, both were sound asleep.

TWO

Just before daybreak on a June morning almost four weeks later, Ashley opened the massive front door of her house and walked outside. She stepped out from the arched entrance and looked at a dawn different from any that she had ever seen. Above the trees, a nearly full moon hung white and ghostly. The rising sun inked the indigo sky with streaks of purple.

She lowered her gaze, glancing along the length of drive that dipped and curved through pooled shadows before reaching the road. That was when she spotted the old Chevy truck and the figure stationed in front of it.

"Vernettie?" she called.

Vernettie stood motionless on the blacktop, her big-knuckled hands thrust into the pockets of a cotton dress that fell straight from her wide shoulders. She stared into the woods on the west side of the property Ashley's parents owned.

Ashley drew her robe around her and walked over to stand beside the old woman. "What are you doing out here at this time of the morning?" she whispered.

"I could ask you the same thing," Vernettie answered. Her breath carried a hint of the raw garlic she chewed each morning, but Ashley didn't mind

11

the odor. It reminded her of when she was younger and Vernettie had hugged her or held her close. Her breath had smelled of garlic then, too.

"What got you up so early?" Vernettie asked. "More bad dreams?"

Ashley nodded. "Plus Nikki," she said. "She woke up crying at four and cried straight through until ten minutes ago." She glanced into the woods, but she didn't see anything that might have caught Vernettie's attention.

"And you didn't want to go back to sleep because the dreams are always worse in the early morning," Vernettie said. It wasn't a question, but a statement.

Ashley shrugged. The dreams hadn't stopped with Nikki's birth, and the four weeks of calm since then hadn't stopped them either. Not all of them were about the young man. If anything, the new dreams were worse, leaving her shaken and pale for hours, even though she was mostly successful in blocking the memory of exactly what she had dreamed.

"So what are you doing outside?" Vernettie asked.

"I came to get the paper."

It was cool for a June morning. Wisps of fog drifted toward them from the creek whose jagged course defined three sides of the property.

The walls of the house, clad in smooth stucco and topped with crenelations like those of a castle, rose behind them. Ashley pulled her hair over her shoulder and twisted it into a single, blond rope. Her bangs felt damp and flat against her forehead. "How long does this colic stuff last, anyway?" she asked, talking to fill up the silence.

"Colic," Vernettie said. She limped to the truck and swung the door shut. "If your parents spent less

12

money on fancy toys for a four-week-old and spent more time holding that baby, they would know that there's something else wrong with her. Something else entirely."

Ashley followed Vernettie to the truck. The ferns that edged the driveway rained drops of dew on her bare ankles. "You don't think Nikki's got colic? What do you think is wrong with her, then?"

As Vernettie faced the stand of trees again, the rising sun colored the sky behind her and haloed her thinning, yellow hair. She breathed deeply, her flat chest rising. "Babies sense things," she said finally. She peered at Ashley. "And so do dreamers," she said.

Goose bumps rose along Ashley's arms. The strange light of this unaccustomed hour, the fog, and Vernettie's intensity were all scaring her.

Vernettie nodded toward the woods. "Do you remember what I told you about my Grandmother Birdie?"

Ashley nodded, a cold dread creeping up from the base of her spine and spreading across her shoulders. "I remember," she said. "She was the one who taught you how to make medicines from the herbs that grow in this part of the country. And she used to know what was going to happen before it happened."

"The herb gathering she could teach me, but soothsaying was different. It can't be taught. I never had the gift for that," Vernettie said. "Only, yesterday, when I was getting in the truck to leave, I thought I heard something up that way. Like a baby squalling. It gave me a bad feeling for Nicole's sake. Like it was an omen."

"It might have been a cat," Ashley said. "Sometimes cats sound like babies." Her shoulders were

13

tensed, hunched forward. She took a deep breath and consciously relaxed them.

Vernettie's mouth worked, changing the pattern of the creases that seamed her face. Flesh sagged in ridges on her neck. "I don't think it was any cat. There was a baby once, before my grandmother's time, who died in mysterious circumstances. Folks used to hear that baby crying long after her death, but Grandmother Birdie, she used to hear the mother screaming for her child."

Vernettie settled her shoulders. "I think something bad's going to happen. And you do, too, don't you? I know you well, Ashley Morgan. You've been thinking it for quite a while, haven't you?"

Ashley walked away from Vernettie, away from the expression in her faded blue eyes. Far down the driveway, near the first curve, a rabbit hopped out of the underbrush. It stopped beside a planting of St. Joseph's Coat, its ears twitching first one direction and then another. After a moment, it sat up with its short forepaws off the ground, then whirled and hopped away.

Ashley made herself turn, exposing her back to the still-dark woods. She glanced up at one of the lighted windows on the second story of the main house— the nursery window—and only then lowered her gaze to look at Vernettie. "This bad thing. Do you think that it has something to do with Nikki?"

"Yes, I do," Vernettie said. She let out a deep breath, then settled her shoulders. "My grandmother quoted me something from the Bible when I was little. Made me memorize it and told me never to forget it. She said I would know when I would need it."

"What was it?" Ashley asked.

14

"For death is come up into our windows, and is entered into our palaces, to cut off the children from without," Vernettie recited. "That quote has been repeating itself inside my head for days now." She shook her shoulders, and then started toward the house. "I just wish I knew what it meant."

She had gone halfway when she stopped, turned toward Ashley, and asked, "You coming in now?"

Ashley shook her head. "I'm going to get the paper first," she said. It seemed as if hours had passed since she had opened the front door and stepped into this strange dawn.

"Suit yourself," Vernettie said, walking past her. "Things look safe enough for now."

The engine of the truck ticked as it cooled. Ashley put her hand on the hood, and felt the warmth of the metal and the slight vibration, as if a giant heart beat there. She glanced at the spot where the rabbit had disappeared into the undergrowth. Something splashed off to the right, where the creek curved closest to the house.

Vernettie could quote passage after passage from the Bible, and often did, but the passage she had chosen this morning seemed particularly disturbing to Ashley. She swallowed, trying to ignore the cold churning in her stomach. For weeks now, she had been trying to convince herself that she had imagined someone waiting for Nikki's birth. Now Vernettie was tying stories about her long-dead grandmother and a colicky baby and Bible verses into one messy prediction that seemed to confirm Ashley's own nagging sense of something wrong.

Then, without warning, a fear as formless as the mist from the creek rose and engulfed Ashley. She stood shivering in its wake for a moment, then turned

15

and hurried toward the house. She left the paper unclaimed somewhere at the far end of the drive.

When she reached the front door, Vernettie waited as if she had expected her to come. "Don't laugh at me," Ashley said, knowing Vernettie would read the panic in her expression.

"I expect I've got more on my mind than laughing at the likes of you," Vernettie said. She touched Ashley's back before closing the door.

THREE

Three days later, Ashley stood at her floor-to-ceiling window. Outside, Lucas and Clay, Vernettie's grandson, walked up the sloping lawn toward the back entrance to the house. Ashley's father had hired both boys to build a gazebo and do lawn care for the summer, and they spent several hours each day on the property. Not only were they building the gazebo: they had helped to design it. Both Lucas and Clay studied architecture in college.

Clay stopped, gesturing with sweeping arm movements toward the foundation of the gazebo. Lucas stood with his hands in his back pockets as he listened. He and Clay were nearly of the same height, but Lucas's build was more muscular and his bone structure heavier than Clay's.

Then, before Ashley had time to move away, Lucas looked up and caught her watching them. He smiled and pointed toward the back of the house. Ashley nodded, understanding that he and Clay were headed inside through the kitchen wing. She started to wave, but then she saw Clay glance from Lucas to her and she lowered her hand.

Dating Lucas had somehow changed her relationship with Clay. Until a few weeks ago, she and Clay had been as close as if he were an older, protective

17

cousin, but he seemed less comfortable with her now. He had always teased her, but she had enjoyed that. Now the teasing had developed an edge that bothered her. Sometimes she even wondered if Clay's feelings for her had been less like that of a cousin and more romantic than either of them had realized.

As Ashley started down the stairs, she heard a car horn beep. She hurried down, stopping as soon as she was level with the top of the first floor windows. She caught flashes of a yellow sports car as it drove past the massive plantings of begonias, St. Joseph's Coats, and vincas that lined the drive near the house. Running down the rest of the stairs, she crossed the foyer. She was waiting on the flagstone walk at the front of the house when Rosamar pulled to a stop.

"Your new car is beautiful," Ashley said when Rosamar opened the door.

As Rosamar got out, her thick, dark hair swung along the line of her jaw. She smiled, one cheek dimpling. "I love it, too," she said, running her hand along the side panel. "That's why I was so late. Once I started driving this morning, I didn't want to stop. I took the long way over."

"Well, you'll get in plenty of driving on the way to the lake. The guys are ready. They just finished up the work for today." She paused, shaking her head. "I can't believe your mother bought this for you."

"Why not?" Rosamar asked, tucking her hair behind one ear. "She bought Lucas one when he turned sixteen, didn't she?"

"Not like this."

"No, but she wasn't a vice president at the bank then, either. Besides, I deserve it, don't I?"

Ashley laughed. "Of course. Your modesty alone

qualifies you to own such an expensive car," she said. "I just wish I could convince my parents that I deserve one like it, too." A breeze lifted her bangs away from her forehead. She turned her face into the wind, breathing in the scents it carried.

"Hold on a sec," Rosamar said, bending into the car. She lifted out a large glass jar filled with something that resembled spaghetti sauce. Holding it up, she said, "My mother's been at it again."

Ashley laughed. "What is it this time?"

"Homemade cream of tomato soup. It has every kind of vegetable known to personkind. Only, trust me. It tastes like tomato juice with milk."

Taking the jar from Rosamar and starting toward the house, Ashley said, "Personkind? Is there such a word?"

Shrugging, Rosamar paused in front of a bed of moss roses. She plucked one of the tiny flowers and threaded the fleshy stem in her hair. "How does it look?" she asked.

"Strange."

"Then maybe it will get you-know-who's attention," Rosamar said. Swinging her keys and gesturing toward the jar, she said, "The more pressure Mother has at the bank, the more she cooks. Not even Lucas can eat it all. And it's all weird stuff like this."

Ashley opened the front door. Light slanted down toward the grey tile floor. "You shouldn't complain. At least she's home often enough to cook. Before Mom had Nikki, she rarely even ate dinner with us, much less cooked it."

Rosamar stopped in front of a row of colorful molas and took a deep breath. "Double chocolate chip cookies," she said.

Ashley shut the door. "I told Vernettie that you were coming."

"Do I have time to eat a couple of dozen cookies before Clay and Lucas get to them?"

"You're too late," Lucas said, walking down the length of the kitchen hallway and emerging into the sunlight that filled the foyer. "Clay and I just polished off the last batch."

"You didn't!" Rosamar said, punching her brother in the arm.

Ashley laughed. Lucas looked at her and smiled.

"No, we didn't eat all the cookies," he told Rosamar. "We just got inside." He leaned over to kiss the bridge of Ashley's nose and then took the jar from her. He held it up and studied its contents. "Isn't this the stuff Mother was cooking last night?" he asked.

"Yes," Rosamar said. "She remembered it just as I was going out the door." Her coloring was darker than Lucas's, her hair a true black while Lucas's was a rich, dark brown. Ashley had fallen into the habit lately of comparing him to the young man from her dreams, and she noted now that his cheekbones were not as prominent, nor his forehead as rounded as the young man's.

Lucas looked down at Ashley. "Vernettie's putting together a picnic basket with enough food for an army," he said. "Maybe we ought to help her."

Ashley hesitated, not sure what to say. Vernettie liked doing things her own way, without interference. Lucas was used to helping in the kitchen. He never seemed to notice Vernettie's irritation.

While Ashley was still thinking of how she might caution Lucas without hurting his feelings, Rosamar jumped in. "I have no intentions of getting in

Vernettie's way and having her snap my head off,'' she said, starting for the kitchen. "But I am going to get some of those cookies. I'm starved.''

When the three of them entered the kitchen, Vernettie was standing near the commercial-sized stove. Clay leaned against the cabinet. His almond-shaped eyes seemed to brighten when they entered the room, but then he looked away. A frown line formed between his brows. Rosamar touched the moss rose in her hair, then lowered her hand.

Vernettie glanced up and saw the jar. "What is it this time?'' she asked, pointing at the jar with a spatula.

"It's homemade soup,'' Rosamar said. Lucas put the jar on the granite countertop.

Sunlight streamed through the stained glass window over the sink and fell in geometric shapes of vibrant blues and reds on the grey tile floor and the bleached cabinet fronts.

"Where's Mom?'' Ashley asked. "I want her to see Rosamar's new car.''

"She's tied up on a phone call. Has been for the last hour.'' Putting down the spatula, Vernettie picked up the jar and twisted the lid.

"I haven't seen the car, either,'' Clay said.

"I'm not leaving this kitchen until I get some cookies,'' Rosamar said, looking at him and then lifting her chin. Ashley almost smiled, but caught herself in time. Rosamar would make Clay pay for not commenting on the flower she wore.

Holding out his hand for the keys, Lucas said, "I'll show the car to Clay. If it's okay.''

Rosamar tossed the keys to Lucas. "Remind me to give you the extra set,'' she said.

21

"Want to come?" Lucas asked Ashley. She glanced at Clay, then shook her head.

At the cabinet, Vernettie took a deep sniff of the soup, then lifted her thin upper lip and said, "Needs salt."

"How can you tell by smelling?" Rosamar asked. She backed up to the cabinet and then swung herself up to sit beside the plate of cookies as easily as if she were mounting the beam in one of her gymnastics competitions.

"Just can," Vernettie answered. She nodded toward the glass of milk that sat on the cabinet near the stove. "Poured you some when I heard your car drive up," she said.

After handing the glass of milk to Rosamar, Ashley drifted to the other side of the kitchen, touching the telephone. "What's going on at the office?" she asked.

"I think that new lawyer fellow that your parents hired to take over some of your mother's cases at the law firm has up and quit," Vernettie said. She crossed the kitchen and dunked the empty cookie sheet into a sinkful of sudsy water. "From what I gather, he's left them in a jam with that big trial coming up."

"Uh oh," Ashley said. "There goes the wonderful summer we had planned." Her mother had been home most days since Nikki's birth, only sitting in occasionally for an important deposition or contract negotiation. She had planned to stay home the rest of the summer.

"Probably so," Vernettie answered without turning around.

Then something strange happened.

The intercom was tuned to the nursery. Ashley was

about to say something else when she heard a low *woosh, woosh* sound coming from the intercom. She listened for her mother's voice, but only heard a wheezing sound. Whoever had just entered the nursery, it hadn't been her mother.

Something made the hair at the nape of her neck rise. "What was that noise?" she asked.

Vernettie paused in the act of washing the cookie sheet and let the sponge drop into the water. She didn't move. She seemed to hold her breath. Then she turned and looked past Ashley.

Ashley could feel the dark length of the kitchen hall stretching out behind her unprotected back. She turned, slowly.

The hall was empty.

Vernettie mumbled something. Ashley caught *window* and *death*.

Her skin went clammy. She didn't have to hear the rest of it to know that Vernettie was repeating the Biblical passage.

Cool air flowed out of the air conditioning vent, fluttering a piece of paper on the bulletin board. For some reason, the movement sent fear trickling down Ashley's spine. She looked at the piece of paper, then up at the intercom.

"Maybe you had best go check on the baby," Vernettie said. Her voice was quiet. "You can get up the stairs faster than I can."

Faster. Suddenly Ashley felt as if the sky had darkened, and night had come, and she was trapped in one of her dreams. She started toward the hallway, walking as if she were wading through a roomful of clear gelatin. Each bump in the stuccoed finish of the walls floated slowly past her line of vision.

Rosamar's voice drifted to her as if from a long

distance. "If Nikki's awake, bring her down so I can see her," she said.

Ashley emerged into the foyer. She could feel the soles of her feet make contact with the insides of her shoes as she stepped down. She could feel the bunching of the muscles in her thighs. Her movements seemed torpid, but her thoughts were racing. She detected an acrid odor—faint, but strong enough to be unpleasant.

"Ashley, did you hear me?" Rosamar asked. She followed Ashley to the bottom of the stairs.

Ashley lifted one foot after the other, climbing tread by tread. She had come to the first landing and had doubled back to head up the second flight of stairs when the stench hit her.

She had never smelled an odor like it, but she knew at once what it was.

It was death.

The awful musk filled the stairway, gagging Ashley.

She leaned over the railing and looked down. Rosamar stood at the foot of the stairs, her figure curiously foreshortened.

Ashley's hand was slick against the railing. She wiped it on the back of her shorts. Every instinct told her to turn and run, but somehow she ascended the stairs, one tread at a time. When she reached the top, she turned to the right, toward the nursery.

Grey carpeting stretched the length of the hall and into the library, all the way to the French doors opened onto the balcony. *For death is come up into our windows,* she repeated to herself as she stared at the glass-paned French doors. She had never noticed how much they resembled windows.

A gust of wind blew through the opened doors, carrying with it the scent of damp leaves and mulch and blooming flowers.

And another scent. One not so fragrant.

Ashley's nostrils flared. The odor was stronger here.

Her heart leaping in her chest, she took several steps. She edged past her own bedroom door, then flattened her back against the wall, hitting the corner of one of the photographs her parents collected. It swung back and forth in a lazy arc. With shaking hands, she stabilized the photograph, and then inched forward, past the bathroom door, only stopping when her left shoulder touched the frame of the nursery door. She waited there, listening. She couldn't bring herself to look just yet.

The strange wheezing was coming from inside the nursery. She could hear it more clearly now.

Something awful was happening inside that room. Ashley realized that she felt fear and dread, but not surprise. Whatever was going on, whatever she would see, she had already seen it in her dreams. And had been so terrified that she had blocked the memory.

Then, from the intercom inside the nursery, she heard Vernettie's voice. "Are you in the nursery?" she asked.

"Not yet," Ashley said. The muscles in her throat had tightened so that her voice was strained. She knew that whoever, or whatever, was in that room, would hear the strain and know that she was afraid.

She couldn't put off the terrible moment of discovery any longer. Taking in a deep breath to steady herself, she stepped around the corner of the door frame and looked into the nursery.

*   *   *

Someone crouched near Nikki's crib. Someone horribly injured.

Ashley registered no more than that before the shock made her feel light-headed. Everything in the room seemed to liquify. The straight lines of the crib, of the windows, and of the corners where wall met wall dissolved into a shifting blackness that dizzied her and made her stomach churn. A sudden cold numbed her hands and feet. The horrible odor fouled the air, so that she could barely draw a breath. She closed her eyes, felt herself sway forward, then caught herself and jerked upright again.

Ashley opened her eyes to a speckled blackness that veiled both the room and the man who bent over Nikki's crib. The room turned, turned, and the blackness grew, spiralling faster and faster as the feeling of déjà vu strengthened. The man in that room must be the other one who had waited for Nikki's birth. Now he had come for her.

Ashley fought to maintain consciousness, but the nausea overpowered her. Trying to shake off the dizziness, she stumbled forward into the nursery. Her last conscious thought was that she had to get to the crib.

She had to see what he had done to Nikki.

FOUR

Ashley opened her eyes.

She thought she must have been dreaming again. She expected to find herself in her bed, with the morning sunlight streaming through her window. Instead she seemed to be lying on the floor. From somewhere nearby, Nikki cried.

At first, Ashley's vision was blurred. She could only make out a series of round shapes that moved against a backdrop of colored spots. Then, straining to focus her eyes, she discovered that a face hovered over hers.

Still under the influence of the dream, she swung her fist up, but Vernettie caught her arm at the wrist. "Hold on," Vernettie said. "It's just me."

Dizziness surged over Ashley, bringing with it a fierce nausea. Her mother's face swam upside down into her line of vision, red-gold curls falling forward to frame her eyes. She held Nikki in her arms and had the portable phone cradled between her shoulder and her ear. "Dr. Varula wants to know if she's conscious now," she told Vernettie over the sound of Nikki's crying.

"Of course, she is," Vernettie said.

Conscious. Not awake, but conscious. It hadn't been a dream then.

As her mother straightened, Ashley caught the swish of the silk lining in her linen slacks. With a sharply indrawn breath, she concentrated on that sound. It reminded her of something, some sound she had heard.

Then she remembered it all. She groaned.

"Let's try sitting you up," Vernettie said.

Black spots swirled through Ashley's vision at the slightest movement, but she was too weak to protest. Lucas must have been standing behind her all the time, because he was with her suddenly, kneeling and lifting her to a sitting position with an arm around her shoulders. She could feel the warmth of his breath on her cheek.

"Better now?" Vernettie asked.

She nodded. She found it difficult to concentrate. Turning her head, she saw Rosamar standing next to Clay in the doorway. Rosamar's complexion was chalky, but she waved at Ashley with a quick, jaunty gesture. "You're going to be okay," she said.

"Dr. Varula said to bring Ashley to the emergency room," her mother said, moving toward the door. Rosamar and Clay stepped out of the way. "She'll meet us there."

"No, wait," Ashley said, struggling to her feet. Lucas steadied her with his hands under her arms.

"There was someone in the room with Nikki," Ashley said. She drew in a breath, and then, without warning, started sobbing. Lucas reached for her, and she went into his arms.

"Ashley," her mother said, her voice a register lower than normal. "Tell me everything that you saw."

"I'm not sure," she said, speaking into Lucas's shoulder. "I thought I saw someone standing by her

28

crib, but then everything started swirling and I got nauseated and he smelled so awful."

No one said anything for a moment. Ashley felt the muscles across Lucas's chest contract as he leaned back to look down at her. She broke away from his embrace and wiped her eyes with both hands.

"Rosamar, you were the first to get to her," Ashley's mother said. "Did you see anyone?"

Rosamar hesitated, then stepped back to the door, her arms still crossed over her chest. "No, Mrs. Morgan," she said. "There *was* a bad smell, but I didn't see anything. I didn't get up here right away. I had gone back to the kitchen to get Vernettie because Ashley was acting strange. Like her brains were scrambled or something. I was talking to her from downstairs and she looked down at me with this blank expression, like she wasn't even seeing me. Vernettie and I found her flat out on the floor."

Ashley looked from Rosamar to Clay. He stood with his arms crossed, looking down at the carpet. What Ashley could see of his face looked flushed with embarrassment.

For me, Ashley thought. He thought she was imagining things.

"There was someone in here and it wasn't a normal person," she said, speaking softly now. She blinked, wanting to cry more than ever, but needing to keep herself under control so that they might believe her.

Lucas took her hand. His eyebrow was cocked up in the familiar, questioning way, but his eyes were sober and there was no smile on his lips.

She looked from him to Vernettie, who met her gaze and didn't look away. After a moment,

Vernettie nodded, the gesture small. Ashley knew what the gesture meant: Vernettie believed her.

"Let me get my purse and we'll take you to the hospital," Ashley's mother said. "Don't worry, Ashley. Dr. Varula said that you might be disoriented. Lucas, would you ride with us in case she faints again?"

"I'm not going to faint," Ashley said. "And I'm not disoriented."

Lucas squeezed her hand. "I want to go with you," he said. "I want to be there."

"Let me hold the baby," Vernettie said, following Ashley's mother into the hall. "There's no sense taking her to the hospital with you."

After handing Nikki to Vernettie, Ashley's mother left the nursery, heading down the hall toward her own bedroom. Her footsteps were silent against the thick carpeting.

Letting go of Lucas's hand, Ashley pushed past Rosamar and Clay without meeting their gazes.

Ashley followed her mother, one hand trailing along the wall to help her keep her balance. She intended to talk to her mother again, but then the sight of the open balcony doors stopped her. Lucas caught up with her there.

"This must be how he got in the house," she said.

She walked onto the balcony, reaching for the railing to brace herself. After scanning the lawn, she looked across the property to the boggy land near the creek. Through the breaks in the trees, she could see where the murky water rose around the knees of the cypresses.

She felt her gaze drawn along the path to the creek. She listened to the sighing of the wind in the trees and she remembered how Vernettie had thought she heard a baby crying out there a few days earlier. Vernettie's words and her warning of death returned with such force that she moaned through closed lips.

"Are you okay?" Lucas asked.

She waited until her breathing steadied. Then, without looking at him, she asked, "You do believe that I saw someone, don't you? Mom didn't. I don't think Clay did, either."

Lucas turned her so that she was facing him. "You've always seemed levelheaded to me, Ash," he said. "I have no reason not to believe you."

Ashley let him draw her into his arms, but, suddenly, she felt an inexplicable anger at him. She wanted him to argue with her. She wanted a chance to convince him and not this too-easy acceptance. Vernettie had believed her, but Vernettie had sensed all along that something was about to happen. She was waiting for it, while the whole thing *must* sound crazy to Lucas. Ought to, at least. She couldn't trust this acceptance of his.

Ashley pulled away from him and turned to scan the property again. "He was there, Lucas," she said, as if he had argued with her. "He was there and he wasn't normal."

"I know," he said.

But he didn't know. He couldn't.

A little more than two hours later, Ashley and her mother returned to the house. Ashley went looking for Vernettie and found her in the kitchen, holding Nikki. Vernettie stood with her back to the stained glass window. Sunlight outlined her skull through her thinning hair.

"What was the doctor's verdict?" Vernettie asked.

"That I have a slight concussion," Ashley said.

31

"I must have hit my head when I fell. They're doing blood tests to find out why I fainted," she said, rolling her eyes. "They think that I might be anemic or something." She touched Nikki's head. Moisture darkened her downy, strawberry blond hair. "I can't believe she's really safe."

Vernettie glanced past Ashley, toward the hallway that led back into the foyer. "Where's your mother?"

"She went upstairs to make some calls."

"And Lucas?"

"We dropped him off at his house. Mom said that I needed to rest."

"And do you?"

Ashley shook her head, then inched her finger under Nikki's palm. When Nikki tightened her grip, Ashley smiled, but then her smile faded. She looked up at Vernettie. "Whoever he was, he was going to kill her, wasn't he?"

Vernettie lifted her shoulders. "That would be my guess," she said.

Ashley slipped her finger out of Nikki's grip.

"Let me get a bottle heated and then we'll talk," Vernettie said, moving away.

The strong light made Ashley's eyes ache. She walked across to the cabinets near the telephone, leaning forward and bracing herself with her hands. While Vernettie put water on to heat and took the bottle from the refrigerator, Ashley studied the row of African violets in front of her. The blossoms were fragile, the leaves like velvet. After a while, she sighed and then straightened. "Who was he?" she asked.

Standing near the stove, Vernettie spoke with hesitation. "I'm not sure. When my grandmother was still alive, she used to tell me that an evil one would

32

come, but that I wasn't to despair, because there would be another one who could stop him." Opening a drawer, she took out a folded cloth. "Put this over your shoulder," she said, holding the cloth out to Ashley.

Ashley took the cloth automatically, glancing down at her sister. "Are you the one who can stop him?" she asked Vernettie.

Vernettie leaned one hip against the kitchen cabinet. Her bony fingers spread across the width of Nikki's back. "No," she said. "I think you're the one Grandmother Birdie meant."

Ashley tried to laugh and found that she couldn't. She turned away, looking past the breakfast area to the oversized chairs grouped around a native stone fireplace. Her muscles suddenly felt weak and unstrung. Her scalp prickled. She wanted to curl up in one of those chairs and pull the cable-knit afghan over her head.

"It's your dreams that make me think that," Vernettie said.

Ashley looked back. "My dreams?" Her lips and tongue felt thick, numbed.

"They're not like other people's," Vernettie said, nodding. "There's more to them. Remember all of those times when you were little and would dream some little thing that ended up really happening?"

Ashley opened her mouth, feeling as if she were suddenly breathing a different and heavier air. In a strange way, she thought that she had somehow expected this conversation all of her life, had been waiting for it and dreading it, and now it had come.

"I started thinking, along about five or six years ago, that maybe you had a gift like my grandmother's," Vernettie said.

The bottle rattled against the bottom of the pan as the water bubbled. Vernettie turned off the burner, then took the bottle out and shook it. Nikki's head bobbed back and forth.

Ashley glanced away, looking through the window. Outside, the pines swayed with the force of the wind. She felt as if that same wind were sweeping through her body. She had always pictured Vernettie's grandmother as a tall, gaunt woman with weathered skin and hair as coarse as straw. A woman who hunted herbs and mushrooms in the virgin forest. And, perhaps, dabbled a little in a bit of harmless witchcraft.

Now Ashley didn't think that she was anything like that.

"Here, if you're steady enough, take your sister," Vernettie said, nodding toward Nikki. When Ashley held her securely, Vernettie met Ashley's gaze over Nikki's head and said, "You know some of the stories about my grandmother, but not all there is to know about her. She was a dreamer. Only, she used her dreams. She said they gave her dream-knowledge."

Somehow Ashley managed to take the bottle from Vernettie and make her way to one of the big chairs near the fireplace. A strange feeling bubbled up through her chest, as if she wanted to cry and laugh at the same time. Something was breaking free inside of her, and, while it caused her pain, she also felt a thrill of exhilaration run through her veins.

She touched the bottle to Nikki's lips, but Nikki refused it, frowning and turning her head away. Ashley placed the bottle on the table beside the chair, then stroked Nikki's brow, more to calm herself than to calm Nikki. The baby's skin was soft and velvety beneath Ashley's fingertips.

Vernettie crossed the room, moving with the slow deliberateness that meant that she was in pain from her arthritis. She remained standing. "It was the sorrow of my life that I didn't have my grandmother's gifts," she said, "but I've started getting reconciled to it. I see what my role could be in life. I'm old now, and nearly crippled, but I can help you. A little, at least. I can tell you the things Grandmother Birdie told me."

"Did your grandmother say why this . . . evil person . . . would want Nikki?" Ashley whispered.

Vernettie shook her head. "I was just a child when she died." She put two fingers across her lips, and then lowered them. "She did say that there are long, in-between times when he doesn't walk the earth. My grandmother lived during one of those times."

Nikki's eyelids quivered as they sank lower. Ashley was overcome by a rush of feelings as the implications of Vernettie's words sank in. She felt love for Nikki, with terror and grief all mixed together with that love. "You mean he's not a real person? He's not alive?"

"My grandmother called him an evil one, a demon," Vernettie said.

Ashley thought that she might vomit. She swallowed against the bitter taste that rose from her throat. "Where is he when he's not . . . walking?" she whispered.

Vernettie bent to rub her thigh just above the knee. When she straightened, her mouth was turned down with sadness, or exhaustion, or pain. She looked toward the front of the house, her eyes seemingly focused on something outside the walls. "Did I ever tell you that I was the youngest child of Grandmother Birdie's youngest child?" she said. "By the time I came along and grew up enough for her to start passing on her knowledge, her voice was already weak. I wasn't sure I was always hearing her right."

"But she said where he was, didn't she?"

Vernettie nodded. "She said in a lair. Like a beast. Out there in the woods."

Ashley stood up so quickly that Nikki woke again, throwing her hands out to either side of her. Vernettie reached out, moving more quickly than Ashley had seen her move in a long time, and gripped Ashley's shoulder, keeping her from running out of the room as she had intended. Vernettie's fingers dug into her skin. "There's danger," she said. "Grandmother Birdie said he would have powers."

Ashley jerked her chin up. "What does that mean?"

"I can't tell you that," Vernettie said, letting her hand drop away from Ashley's shoulder. "There's all kind of demon powers. The power to read minds. Dominion over the animals. The power to foretell the future or change shapes."

Ashley started to turn away, but Vernettie spoke to her. "But you're not without powers of your own, Ashley Morgan," she said. "You have the dream-knowledge, if only you didn't hide it from yourself. Probably, that's why he waited this five weeks to come after Nicole. He was waiting to see what you would do against him."

"Nothing," Ashley whispered, looking into Vernettie's face. "I did nothing. And now he'll come back."

Vernettie pursed her lips, deep lines radiating out from her mouth. Then she shook her head. "I don't understand it, but either there's some harm you can still do to him or else there's some other reason he can't touch her yet. Else he would have taken Nicole with him today. There wasn't anybody up there to stop him. Now it's up to you to figure out what it is that will stop him.''

Up to her? Ashley looked down at the baby she cradled in her arms. Nikki blinked, and then her eyes closed again, but Ashley could see the back-and-forth movement of her eyes beneath the nearly transparent skin of her eyelids. Bending forward, Ashley kissed each eyebrow. Then she raised her head. "How?" she asked. "How do I find out what to do?''

"There's only one way for you to do it that I can figure out,'' Vernettie answered. "And that's by dreaming it.''

That night, Ashley lay for a long time with her legs straight and her arms down by her sides. She stared out the window, trying to ease herself into sleep. She had always hated times when she didn't know what to do, how to act. She liked to plan out her days and her life, and she liked as little conflict as possible. Now she willed herself to dream of the demon and to remember the dream.

When she finally dropped off, despite her resolution, she did not dream of a way to stop the demon. Instead she dreamed of the young man dying in the mud-walled room. His thirst scorched her throat as she watched his body twist first to one side and then to the other. In her own bed, she drew her legs up in response to the pain in his stomach.

There was the sound of bare feet moving across the hard-packed dirt floor of the outer room. The young man turned his head toward the opening. He could tell from the charged feeling in the air that the person approaching was the one for whom he had sent.

He had been prepared for what he would see, but still he flinched from the monstrous man who appeared in the doorway. A crushing blow to his skull some time long ago had left it dented in above the left eye. The eye itself was missing and the socket empty. His withered left arm ended just above the elbow, the flesh tapering and then flaring out into a reddened knot. A woman attended him. He leaned on her shoulder, hobbling into the room. Although both feet were whole, the right one seemed not to flex at the joint.

As the young man watched the older one advance, his fever-glazed eyes widened. Pain seared through his mid-section. "Help me," he whispered through clamped-together teeth.

Ashley woke. She lay gasping, her knees drawn up to her chest and her hands pressed against her stomach. Gradually the phantom pain left her. She straightened her legs and wiped away the tears from the corners of her eyes. After a moment, she kicked off her covers and rose to complete her nightly ritual of checking the windows and doors.

FIVE

The next afternoon, Ashley sat beside Lucas on a sandy bank and glanced across the water of Lake Conroe. Clay and Rosamar had rented a Sunfish and were tacking slowly toward the landing farther down the shore. The tatters of white clouds along the horizon made the rest of the sky appear a more intense blue by comparison.

Ashley leaned back and tilted her face up to the sky. This was the first time that she and Lucas had been alone all day. She sensed that he was waiting to talk to her, but so far she had managed to avoid any serious discussion. For just a few moments longer, she wanted to pretend that it was weeks earlier, when she and Lucas had first started dating and their friendship had begun changing into something else. She wanted to pretend that she had nothing but romance on her mind.

"Clay's acting strangely today," she said, glancing at Lucas. "Did you notice the way that he hustled Rosamar into the Sunfish after she said she didn't want to go out on the lake?"

Lucas smiled.

She loved his eyes. They were a rich brown with hazel flecks that only showed up in sunlight this strong. She looked at them, then remembered the dark eyes of the young man in her dream, his pupils expanded because of the fever.

"He was pretty obvious, wasn't he?" Lucas said.

It took Ashley a moment to remember that they were discussing Clay. "Do you think that he's finally getting interested in Rosamar?" she asked.

Lucas touched her hand. "No. He wants me to talk to you. Alone."

Ashley sat up. Her arms and legs felt weighted, and without the delicious laziness that usually went along with the summer heat.

"He's been worried about his grandmother for a while now," Lucas said. "He thinks that she may be responsible for what happened yesterday."

"What do you mean, responsible? Vernettie wasn't even upstairs when it happened."

"Not responsible that way. Vernettie's stories can be more than a little persuasive. One night a few years ago, Clay and I spent the night at her house. She told some ghost stories that set our hair on end. We all know that you have a soft spot for Vernettie. Clay thinks that she may have influenced you more than you realize."

"If that's what he thinks, then why didn't he tell me himself?"

"Maybe he thought that you would listen to me more than you would listen to him," Lucas said. "I was kind of flattered, to tell the truth. Things have been a little rocky between me and Clay lately. You can guess why."

Ashley felt her face flush. She looked away, out over the water.

"I haven't had the heart to tell Rosie," Lucas said.

Ashley smiled at that. "Don't you worry about Rosamar," she said. "She likes challenges."

Looking down into her eyes, Lucas laughed. He leaned toward her.

Thinking that he might be about to kiss her, Ashley straightened. There was something that she had to get straight first. "Do you agree with Clay?" she asked. "Do you think that I'm imagining all of this because of stories that Vernettie's told me in the past?"

Lucas squeezed Ashley's hand, but he hesitated an instant too long before saying, "No, that's not what I think."

"But you don't really believe that I saw anyone in the nursery," Ashley said, making it a statement and not a question.

Lucas didn't answer.

Ashley took in a deep breath. "You were pretending to believe me yesterday, weren't you? I hate it when people pretend to believe something that they don't believe."

He looked at her then, meeting her gaze steadily. "Sometimes what you call *pretending* isn't pretending, Ash. Sometimes it's trusting even when something's hard to believe. I trust you."

Two young girls ran up to the edge of the bank and then jumped into the water, splashing Ashley and Lucas. Both girls carried water guns that they pointed at each other. One had hair nearly the exact color of Nikki's, and it was nearly as wispy, too.

Looking at her, Ashley's hands went clammy. "I'm afraid, Lucas," she said. All day she had been trying to remember precisely what she had seen when she first looked into the nursery, but she had grown so practiced at suppressing anything that frightened

41

her that she couldn't remember. All that remained was the hazy outline of someone bending over Nikki's crib and the conviction that something had been terribly wrong with him.

"What do you think is going to happen?" Lucas asked.

"I think the man is going to come back, and that, when he does, he's going to kill Nikki."

Ashley had intended to make her voice firm, but she hadn't realized how loudly she had spoken. When she looked up, she saw that the two girls stared at her, their eyes round and their eyebrows lifted. They stood knee-deep in the water. Then their gaze shifted to something behind Ashley.

Ashley felt her blood go cold with fright. She whirled around, but it wasn't the man from the nursery who stood behind her, but only Rosamar and Clay.

Rosamar tilted her head back to look up at Clay, who shook his head, then walked back toward where they had parked the car.

Putting her hands on her hips, Rosamar turned back to Ashley. "Now look what you've done," she said. "You've gone and distracted him just when he was finally starting to notice how good I look in this bathing suit."

No one swam or went out in the Sunfish for the rest of the afternoon. Ashley and the others spread a quilt beneath a grouping of pines that stood back from the shore, where there would be enough privacy to talk without being overheard. Clay sat with his back against a tree, and his long, slim legs extended in front of him. His eyes were narrowed so that the blue of his irises barely showed. Rosamar knelt across from him, and Lucas sat between his sister and Ashley.

"Look at Clay," Rosamar said, leaning back to whisper to Ashley behind Lucas's back. "A whole day of all-out flirting absolutely wasted."

Ashley smiled for a moment, then sat forward again. Rosamar leaned forward, shrugged, and then said, "I called Vernettie at her place last night, after she left your house."

Ashley had thought that she knew Rosamar well enough not to be surprised at anything she did, but this surprised her. "Why did you call her?" she asked.

"Because everything felt so weird," Rosamar answered. "Vernettie told me about your talk. About your dreams. About her grandmother, too."

Ashley's face flushed with warmth. She glanced at Lucas and then at Clay. "Vernettie had no right to tell that to anyone else," she said.

"I told you that this was Grandma Vernettie's doings," Clay said, speaking to Lucas. He settled against the tree, tilting his head back and looking at them along the length of his nose, the way Ashley had seen him look at Vernettie when she got started on one of her tales.

"Let them talk," Lucas said.

Clay lifted his hands, palms up. "I'm not stopping them, am I?" he asked.

Lucas looked at Ashley. Over his shoulder and beyond where Rosamar sat, she saw a group of people setting up a volleyball net. She wished they could all go over and join them and forget everything else.

"What's this about dreams?" Lucas asked.

Ashley breathed in, glancing at Clay. "The dreams aren't important."

"Maybe they are," Rosamar said, leaning forward and touching her brother's arm to get his attention. "Lucas, remember? I've told you before about Ashley's dreams and how some of them come true."

"I don't want to talk about this any more," Ashley said, glancing at Clay. "My dreams don't have anything to do with what I saw yesterday."

Rosamar ignored her. She scooted forward and knelt in front of Lucas. "Vernettie said that Ashley thinks someone's been watching the house for a long time," Rosamar told her brother. "Since before Nicole was born."

Clay moved his feet, drawing them up and bending his knees. "This is crazy," he said. "There's nothing to be worried about, except the state of my grandmother's mental health," he said. "I love her, but she's beginning to go off the deep end. Be logical. If there were anybody hanging around and spying on people, don't you think Lucas and I would have noticed some signs around the place?" he asked, watching Ashley.

"Be logical yourself, Clay Blackshear," Rosamar said. "I doubt if he would hang around in daylight."

"No, but if someone were wandering around at night, sooner or later he would step in one of the flower beds. That, or leave a soft drink can or cigarette butts lying around somewhere. There'd be something, somewhere."

"There's nothing to stop us from searching the woods near the house just to rule out the possibility, is there?" Lucas asked. "If it would make Ashley feel better?"

"Yes, there is a reason," Clay said. "It would just give this whole thing more importance than it ought to have." He pulled off the baseball cap he wore and then resettled it on his head.

44

Ashley shook her head. "No, I think it's a good idea," she said. "We ought to search. But not just to make me feel better. To prove to all of you that I'm right." She looked up, and then back down at the quilt. She rubbed a burn scar on the back of her thumb, feeling the ridge of healed scar tissue under the skin.

"I'll go with you guys," Rosamar said. She gave Clay a look, her eyebrows raised in a way that reminded Ashley of Lucas.

Clay let out a long breath of air that might have been a sigh. "Okay. I'll go, too," he said. "But don't say I didn't tell you so when it turns out to be a wasted trip."

"Thanks," Ashley said, looking at each of them in turn. She leaned over, opening the picnic basket. "Let's eat," she said.

Then she sat on her heels, thinking. Sweat beaded her upper lip. Her stomach did flipflops. She had the feeling that very soon she was going to wish that this trek through the woods had never been planned.

Near eleven that evening, Ashley stood in her room and looked down at the bassinet that she had moved to the side of her bed. The soft glow of a nightlight provided the room's only illumination.

Nikki lay on her stomach, her head turned to the side. Her cheeks dimpled and then released as she sucked on her pacifier. Her downy hair fluffed away from her scalp, and one hand opened and closed on the sheet, her thin nails making scratching sounds. Ashley shivered when the air-conditioning duct sent a cold draft down the back of her neck. Sunburned skin tightened across her shoulders and upper arms. She had forgotten to wear sunscreen at the lake that day.

She tucked the receiving blanket around Nikki's

shoulders, and then walked across the room to stand near the window, gazing out at the landscape. A lop-sided moon hung low over the trees, throwing shadows across the lawn. Ashley studied the shadows, then whispered, "We're coming to find you. Tomorrow."

"Who are you talking to?" her father whispered from the doorway of her room.

"Oh!" Ashley said, turning and facing him. "Nothing. No one."

Her father walked into the room and bent over the bassinet. "So you're taking over the feedings for tonight," he said, reaching toward Nikki.

Watching him, an image flashed in Ashley's memory. Her eyes narrowed. Another hand had reached for Nikki, moving in that same way, reaching out with curved fingers. But when Ashley tried to remember more, just how the hand had looked rather than the way it had moved, the image evaporated. It left nothing behind but the aftershocks along the paths of her nerves.

Her father straightened and then walked toward her. Ashley turned away and faced the window.

"It's beautiful out there tonight, isn't it?" he asked. "I wish I knew enough about photography to do it justice."

Ashley glanced at him, and then back to the window. Sometimes she wondered if he would have been happier as an artist than as a lawyer. If he felt the same way, he never mentioned it. "Dad," she said, "I keep remembering bits and pieces of what I saw the day before yesterday. It scares me."

Her father put his hands on her shoulders and massaged the base of her neck with his thumbs. Ashley tilted her head forward, trying to relax her muscles despite the soreness in her sunburned skin.

Nikki sighed, and then gave a sudden cry. Ashley's father broke away and moved to the bassinet. "It's okay," he said. "Somehow she managed to turn herself onto her back."

He turned Nikki onto her stomach again, gave her the pacifier, and began patting her back.

It was somehow easier for Ashley to talk now that her father wasn't standing so close. "I did see someone in the nursery," she said.

"No one else saw anything, Ash," her father said. A lock of his hair, almost colorless in this light, fell over his forehead. He stopped patting Nikki and held his hand inches above her back.

"Dad?" Ashley asked.

Her father looked at her across the width of the room. A swath of moonlight separated them.

"Lucas and the others promised to help me look for signs that someone's been hanging around. We're going tomorrow. Would you come with us?"

Her father sighed. "I've already looked," he said.

"You looked? When?"

"The afternoon it happened."

So he had believed her. At least a little. Something warmed in the center of Ashley's chest.

He must have noticed a change in her expression. Shaking his head, he said, "I didn't find anything. No footprints anywhere around. No signs that anyone's been trying to force their way into the house. Nothing. There wasn't anyone here, Ash. People don't shinny up the sides of houses and then jump off a balcony without leaving some kind of sign."

"People don't, but what if he's not a person?"

Ashley hadn't meant to say that, but her own words rang in her ears in a way that made her pay

47

attention to them. Maybe he wasn't a person. Grand-mother Birdie had called him an evil one, a demon.

But he had hands. And a human form.

Ashley's father stepped forward into the moonlight. His blond hair and brows shone in the light. He stood still, his long arms at his sides, his eyes narrowed as he watched Ashley. She forced herself to laugh. "I'd better go to bed," she said. "I'm so sleepy that I'm starting to talk crazy."

Her father breathed in. His shoulders relaxed. "It was probably too much for you, going out to the lake today while you were still recuperating from the concussion. Are you sure you don't want your mother and I to take Nicole tonight?"

"No, you both have to go to work early. I can do it."

Her father came over to her, looked at her for a moment, and then kissed her forehead. "Want us to leave the intercom on?" he asked.

Ashley nodded. "Sure," she said. "That would be a good idea. In case I don't wake up right away if Nikki cries."

Her father left her then, but he stopped in the threshold of her door. "This won't go on too much longer," he said. "Your mother's going to call the agency tomorrow and see if the nanny can start sooner than we told them originally." He tapped the door frame once and then left the room.

Ashley's lips went cold. The nanny. Once the nanny came, she would take over Nikki's care.

Only what protection would a dreamless nanny provide against someone who maybe wasn't a person, but had a person's hands and a human form?

SIX

Late the next afternoon, Ashley went downstairs and out the front door. Waving to Lucas and Clay, who were working near the storage shed, she walked across to Vernettie's truck and stood leaning against it. A breeze blew across the drive and lifted her bangs.

It was nearly time. Rosamar should arrive at any moment.

Ashley slipped off one sandal. There was a light coating of sand on the edge of the asphalt drive, reminding her of the sandy bank at the lake. She moved her foot back and forth, watching the ridges her toes made, as she tried to keep herself awake. Most of the night before, she had kept herself from falling into a deep sleep. She had dreaded soft footsteps moving down the hall in the dark, and she had dreaded the dreams.

Birdsong sounded all through the woods, but she barely registered what she heard. The trees rustled in the breeze. She could smell the hot asphalt, the bitter scent of yellow marigolds that edged the bed nearby, the rich, complex smells of the woods themselves. She concentrated on the odors to reassure herself that she was still awake.

A car pulled onto the drive. Ashley's hand trembled when she lifted it to brush a strand of hair out of her face. A fine sheen of sweat broke out on her face and chest.

Rosamar parked her car and opened the door. She was pale, but dressed in a brightly flowered shirt and khaki-colored shorts. Ashley looked across to the storage shed where Clay was putting the lawnmower away. Lucas had been emptying sacks of clippings into the composter, but he turned and caught her glance. Just then Vernettie opened the front door, walking out onto the flagstone walkway.

"Let's get this show on the road," Rosamar said.

A high, keening sound like the whine of a siren began in Ashley's head. The sky darkened as a cloud rolled in front of the sun.

She pushed away from the truck, her head swimming with the change in position. "You'll make sure that Nikki's not left alone?" she asked Vernettie, meaning not just for that day but for all the days to come. For some reason, this excursion into the woods frightened her more than anything else that she had ever done. She didn't know what might happen, and she hated that feeling. Still, she felt as if she had no choice but to do it. She was going to have to face the dreams soon, and she was going to have to face this trek into the woods today.

Vernettie nodded. Her lips were tight, her nostrils pinched. "You look like you're about to pitch over face first onto the driveway. You didn't sleep any last night, did you?"

Ashley looked at her for a long moment. "I'll sleep tonight," she said. "I hope."

Then, turning, she was the first of the group to enter the woods.

* * *

Ashley scanned the ground on either side of her as she walked, then looked up into the branches of the trees. Brambles reached across the path that she and the others had chosen, snagging her socks. When she paused to pull them away, she noticed that the needles of a pine tree nearby had thickened grotesquely, forming clots of green high up in the branches.

The air was hot and still and seemed depleted of oxygen. Lucas wiped the sweat from his eyes with the back of his arm.

"Boo!" Clay whispered, leaning toward Ashley.

"Go back if you're not going to be serious," she said. She glanced into the tree a last time and then away.

Clay took off his cap and pushed his hand through his hair. "Okay, I'm serious," he said, putting the cap on again. "Where exactly are we headed? Shouldn't we just be going around the edges of the woods if this guy's supposed to be watching the house?"

Lucas edged closer to Ashley. She looked up at him, then at Clay. "No," she said. "I want to look farther back."

"Okay," Clay said. "If that's what you want. There's a clearing of sorts back in this direction. Why don't we start there and then fan out?"

They didn't pause again until they were at the edge of the clearing. Ashley was more exhausted from lack of sleep than she had thought. Her arms and legs seemed unnaturally heavy. Her eyes burned and itched.

In the clearing, a thin covering of scraggly grass grew over the red dirt. An old-fashioned hydrangea grew against a pile of rubble, the pink blossoms full and round.

A sudden breeze caught the live oak, shivering the deep green leaves and drawing her attention. She held her breath, watching as a strange wind circled the clearing, enclosing her and the others in a ring of swaying branches. She stepped forward, listening to the voice of the wind sigh and moan as it moved through pine and sweet gum and dogwood and live oak. A sudden cold slowed her heartbeat and numbed her throat so that she couldn't swallow the saliva that filled her mouth.

Lucas and Clay conferred over something, but their voices were strangely distant. Ashley started to turn toward them, to tell them that she was dizzy and needed to sit down, but as soon as she turned, she was struck with a compulsion to look back.

A cabin stood in the clearing. Its door was open.

Ashley shook her head to clear it. The trees rustled with a sighing sound that seemed to echo her own breaths, as if she were enclosed within a giant lung.

When she looked again, the cabin was still there. The late afternoon sun painted its wood a vibrant color.

Then the breeze died as suddenly as it had begun. The sun broke through a cloud. The air seemed unbearably hot. The heat added to Ashley's confusion. Her legs and arms felt swollen and heavy. Sweat broke out along her upper lip and plastered her T-shirt to her chest. It seemed an immense effort to move, but she looked toward where she had left the others standing.

They were gone.

*   *   *

Ashley turned in a full circle, but Lucas, Rosamar, and Clay had disappeared.

A wave of dizziness washed over her, as if the whole world had tilted and she were sliding down into unreality, helpless to stop. She held out her hands to steady herself, then turned back to the cabin.

Its inset window held no glass. A cloth covered the opening, but the cloth had been pulled to the side. The wooden planks looked newly sawn. The hydrangea bush looked smaller than it had when Ashley had spotted it only a few moments earlier. Now it appeared to be in its first blooming. Ashley sank to her knees, trying to understand what she was seeing.

"Lucas, where are you?" she whispered.

She felt hands on her shoulders, shaking her. She looked up, expecting to see Lucas, tears of relief gathering in her eyes.

Only there was no one standing near her.

She shuddered with fear. A voice rumbled, as if it were transmitted through a wall, but she recognized its timbre, its rhythm. She felt a pressure across her shoulders that was somehow both familiar and comforting.

"Lucas?" she asked.

She staggered to her feet. Unseen hands helped her, supported her when her legs threatened to give way again. She tried to speak, but her tongue moved thickly against the roof of her mouth. She felt herself being urged back. She turned toward the path in response to a pressure at the small of her back.

The path was gone.

A tall pine whose first branches began twenty feet above the ground stood where the path should have opened into the clearing.

One hand to her mouth, Ashley broke away from

the hands supporting her. What she was seeing was a hallucination. All of it. It had to be. Sweat ran in a line down the middle of her back, soaking the waistband of her shorts. Her socks were damp and soggy. She wiped perspiration from her forehead, trying to think.

Then she heard a woman singing, the voice clear and not rumbling, as Lucas's had been.

Startled, she turned in the direction of a new path, one that led toward the creek. A woman walked up the path toward her. She wore a white, high-necked, collarless blouse that buttoned up the front and a full, loose skirt that ended only an inch above her ankles.

Ashley made a sound deep in her throat, but the woman didn't react. She didn't seem to see Ashley or hear her. She continued toward the clearing. Ashley reached out to either side and felt her hands grasped. She tried to steady her breathing and pay attention to what was happening.

The woman was slender and her bare feet were narrow, long, and slightly flat. Her dark hair was parted in the middle and drawn back underneath her bonnet. She wore no makeup, but the heat of the day had brightened her cheeks and lips. She carried a basket full of wet laundry. She was smiling. Turning, Ashley followed the woman's movements as she crossed to the other side of the clearing.

The woman sat the basket on the ground. Bending down, she lifted a garment from the pile of clothing, then spread it across the branches of a bush near the edge of the clearing.

That was when Ashley noted what type of garment it was.

It was a diaper.

*　　*　　*

54

Ashley's long, indrawn breath deepened into a groan. "She has a baby," she whispered to the protecting hands. Her gaze went to the open cabin door.

Just then, something slid across the plank floor of the cabin. Something too far back in the dark interior to be seen. Something not a baby, but larger, heavier.

The young woman heard it, too. She paused for only an instant, her head tilted to the side. Then she started for the open door, her dark brows drawn together. Watching, Ashley understood what the woman did not. It was already too late. Too late to save her baby. Ashley felt as if all of her blood had pooled in her heart, expanding it until she couldn't breathe.

She looked back at the door. A dead blackness seemed to absorb all the light.

A dead blackness with a human silhouette.

Before Ashley could move, the dark mass advanced, catching the afternoon light that slanted low over the trees.

The man that Ashley had seen in Nikki's bedroom now stood in the doorway of the cabin.

"O-o-oh," the woman said, her voice rising and then falling in a way that was almost comical.

Although Ashley had suppressed her memory of the man in the nursery, she recognized him now. She remembered the charred-looking skin that stretched thinly over wasted muscles. Seeing the look of that skin again, she realized what must be wrong with him.

He must have been horribly burned.

Then she wasn't sure. A bitter taste rose to the back of her throat as she looked at a place along his neck where his skin had split, revealing dessicated flesh that was an ugly purple in color.

Breaking away from the protecting hands, Ashley staggered to the edge of the clearing. Determined not to faint again, she clung to the trunk of a pine sapling, the ragged edges of the bark pressing into the flesh of her upper arm. The taste of bile rose to the back of her throat. She couldn't swallow, couldn't make the muscles in her throat function. Behind her, the woman wept and murmured something over and over.

Steeling herself, Ashley looked again. She noted that the man's matted hair had pulled away in clumps.

He wasn't burned. Something else was wrong with him, something . . . And then, Ashley saw what he held in his arms.

"The baby," she whispered. "He has the baby."

Thickened fingernails dented the baby's soft flesh.

"Elizabeth," the woman sobbed, falling forward onto all fours.

Ashley's knees buckled. Once again the supporting hands lifted her. Her friends tried to urge her away with hands and rumbling voices, but she clung to the tree.

"Give me my baby," Elizabeth's mother pleaded.

The man turned his face toward Elizabeth's mother. He started toward her, his bones grating together as if they were dry sticks. One of Elizabeth's arms was flexed at the elbow, fingers half-curled in a cruel imitation of the relaxed posture of a sleeping infant. There was something wrong in the color of her skin. It was a dark blush that deepened to purple at her fingertips.

Ashley swayed, clinging to the tree.

She understood, finally, that she was seeing something that had happened in the past. Elizabeth's mother must be the woman Vernettie had told her about, the one whose baby had died in some mysterious way before Grandmother Birdie had moved to this part of the country, the one Grandmother Birdie had heard screaming.

Pine needles stuck to the soles of the man's feet, plastered there by the thick weeping of the seams that had opened in his flesh. As he walked, Elizabeth's limbs moved as if swayed by a gentle breeze.

He drew closer to the woman. She rose onto her hands and knees, grabbing his leg. Ashley had time to register that Elizabeth's eyes were open and that they were blue and that her head was tilted back at an unnatural angle, but then the man pressed the infant's body closer to his chest, and her face was hidden. He pulled away from the woman, who was left sitting on the ground, her mouth gaping open.

The only sounds Ashley heard were the rasping of his breath, the sobbing of Elizabeth's mother, and her own hoarse sobs.

Then the man opened his arms. Ashley tried to scream, but couldn't draw enough breath. Elizabeth's body tumbled down, the fall seeming to last long minutes, and then she landed on the ground with a thud that sickened Ashley. Ashley heard screaming then, and thought that she might be the one screaming, but it was Elizabeth's mother. Elizabeth's body lay on its side, the face turned toward Ashley, one hand splayed on the sand, palm down.

Not even the supporting hands could hold Ashley upright then. She sank down, squatting on the ground with her hands braced on the ground in front of her.

Elizabeth's fingertips and toes were a deep purply-black to the first joint. Her eyes were open, but had already lost their moisture and had shrunken in their sockets.

But it wasn't her eyes or her black fingers and toes that made Ashley leap to her feet and run away.

It was Elizabeth's mouth. Elizabeth's mouth with her swollen tongue protruding from between her lips. With shreds of putrid flesh clinging to those purpled lips.

Ashley ran into the woods, ducking under branches that barred her way. Brambles slashed her legs. A vine the thickness of her wrist snaked across her path. She stumbled, fell, then scrambled to her hands and knees. She got to her feet again, her heart thundering in her chest.

Nothing seemed to be in its right place. Trees grew where the path should have been. She ran past a thickly wooded rise on which their house should have been standing, but wasn't. She doubted her own senses.

For a while, she heard the woman's screams, but as she ran farther the sound thinned until Ashley heard only her own ragged breathing. It scarcely seemed human.

She ran on until she lost all track of time or place, not even sure whether she might have crossed the same territory over and over again. She couldn't orient herself.

Her lungs burned. Her chest was on fire. Slowing to a jog, she stumbled across a rotting tree.

And found herself on the edge of empty space.

She swayed forward over a steep bank. Her heart seemed to stop. She went cold in the pit of her stomach. Then she managed to pull up short without toppling over the edge. Below her, two dead fish that were each the length of her thumb lay on the cracked mud that floored the dry bed of a creek.

Her chest heaving, she staggered around a tree that grew close to the bank, its roots hanging raggedly out of the steep sides, and saw a stone dam ahead of her. She breathed in great noisy gasps, her hands on her chest.

She recognized where she was. The dam that spanned the creek's width was on their property, somewhere between a half mile and a mile from their house. She had walked through here before.

Or had she? The dam looked different. The stones seemed rougher and more uneven than she remembered them being. She backed away, stopping at the tree growing near the bank. She glanced back. No mosses or algae softened the outline of the stones, as they had the last time she had seen the dam.

Sitting on the ground, she settled herself with her back against the tree, her feet drawn up. She looked back in the direction from which she had come, thinking of Elizabeth's mother alone at the cabin with that man and with Elizabeth's body. She couldn't hear screaming any longer. Perhaps the man had gone away now that he had killed Elizabeth, and Elizabeth's mother was holding her dead baby, crooning a lullaby that Elizabeth wouldn't hear.

The air was heavy with moisture. Ashley's muscles felt liquid, as if they might never support her weight again. Sweat ran into the scratches from the briars, stinging her legs. She accepted her exhaustion gratefully, sinking into it.

Sometime later a rattling sound woke her.

She opened her eyes. At first, she saw nothing but the crumbling dirt walls that had somehow wrapped themselves around her, the dried leaves that cushioned her.

Then she looked up at the rim of the shallow, leaf-filled basin in which she was lying.

What she saw when she looked up set her heart beating fast against her ribcage.

A snake was coiled on the rim of the basin, only inches from her face.

60

SEVEN

"Don't move," Lucas said from somewhere nearby, his voice so low that Ashley barely heard him. The rim of the basin blocked her view, but his voice no longer rumbled, and she could distinguish his words.

A twig pressed into the flesh of her cheek, making the muscle twitch. She stared at the snake, mesmerized by its big, blunt head and by the flicking of its tongue.

The snake coiled its body, its head poised to strike. The shiver of its muscles hypnotized Ashley. She would not have been able to move even if Lucas hadn't warned her. A snake used its tongue to taste the air, she knew.

It was tasting her scent.

If it struck her on the face, how long would it take the venom to get to her heart and brain?

"Lucas, I love you," she whispered.

Clay cursed under his breath. His whispered syllables mimicked the buzzing of the snake's rattles. Until he had spoken, Ashley hadn't known that he was with Lucas.

"Don't go saying your last words," Clay told her. "We're going to get you out of there."

"Careful, Lucas!" she heard Rosamar cry from somewhere out of her view.

Ashley heard the rustle of footsteps on dry leaves. Moving so quickly that Ashley could scarcely register the motion, the snake twisted, reforming its coils, its tongue flicking in the direction of Lucas's voice.

Ashley lifted her head.

"Don't move!" Clay barked. "Don't move until one of us tells you to."

Lucas crept into Ashley's view, his knees flexed and his arms loose at his sides. The snake vibrated its tail, increasing the pitch of its rattle. The lowest coil of its body hung over the lip of the depression, only inches from Ashley's head.

Suddenly the rattler drove its head and upper body toward Lucas.

Ashley screamed, sitting up as Lucas flung himself backward, out of range of the blunt, striking head. In that instant, when the rattler's body was extended to its fullest, Clay jumped forward, his booted foot landing across the snake's body.

Before Ashley could scream again or scramble out of the basin, the rattler twisted, sinking its fangs into Clay's boot.

Clay kicked, flinging the snake away, its body rolling as it twisted through the air. It hit the ground somewhere in the brush, out of Ashley's sight. There was a rustling that seemed to go on forever, and then silence.

Ashley sat where she was. A cold sweat prickled her upper lip, her underarms, and the middle of her back.

Lucas reached down toward her. Taking his extended hand, she let him pull her to her feet and then into his arms. He kissed her forehead first and then her lips.

His cheeks were a dull red. The front of his T-shirt was soaked with sweat. Ashley's heart beat with uneven rhythm as she lay against his shoulder. She turned her head to look at the others. Rosamar had a scratch across her face and one on her leg. Clay stood behind Rosamar, his chest heaving.

Lucas and Clay had both risked their lives to save her, but it was Clay whom the snake had attacked. "Are you all right?" she asked him, her voice raw and harsh.

"Yes, it just got my boot, but that was too damn close," he said, bending over and examining his boot. He straightened. "Don't you know better than to lie down in a pit full of leaves like that?"

Ashley pulled away from Lucas. "I didn't," she said. "I was leaning against that tree, and I must have fallen over." She turned, pointing.

There was no tree growing near the basin.

Rosamar walked over to stand beside Ashley and Lucas. She looked down into the shallow basin. "There could have been a tree here once, I guess," she said. "Its roots could have torn out this chunk of dirt when the tree fell." She took a few steps around the perimeter of the basin. "But we're talking about something that happened a long time ago. The trunk's completely rotted away."

Ashley stepped back and brushed leaves and bits of twigs from her clothing. She had no answer that would make sense to Rosamar or the others. She was sure that there had been a tree. She could even remember the imprint of the bark against her back when she had leaned against it.

"Lucas?" Rosamar asked, still looking down into the basin. "Is it possible that . . . ?"

Lucas waited. "That what?" he asked.

Rosamar looked up, a frown line between her brows. She shook her head. "Nothing," she said. She turned to Ashley. "You're not hurt or anything, are you?" she asked. "We really ought to get back. It'll be dark soon."

"I'm fine," Ashley said, looking around. Deep shadows lay beneath the canopy of trees. "I must have lost track of time," she said. "How long has it been since we first came into the woods?"

When Rosamar didn't answer, and neither did any of the others, Ashley looked at Lucas. He met her gaze for a moment, his eyes sober. "Several hours," he finally answered. "You got away from us when you ran out of the clearing. We couldn't find you anywhere." There was a twig caught in his dark hair, she noticed.

"How much could you see of what was happening in the clearing?" she asked. "Did you see the man? Or the cabin? Or Elizabeth and her mother?"

Clay blew out a long breath, but he wouldn't meet her gaze. "We didn't see anything," he said. "Or hear anything. Except what you were saying."

Ashley's cheeks flushed, and she looked down at the ground. They had been watching her as she reacted with horror to something they couldn't see. As she spoke to a person who didn't seem to exist. She had told them she was leaning against a tree that seemed to have fallen down and rotted away while she slept. She could imagine what they thought of her.

As if Lucas guessed the turn that her thoughts had taken, he cupped her chin, turning her face up toward his. "I could feel you trembling when I touched you. Your voice was . . . I don't know how to describe it, but I couldn't stand hearing it."

"I was seeing something horrible, Lucas," she said.

"What?" he asked. His eyes were warm and calm and concerned. Ashley needed both those qualities just now.

She looked into his eyes for a moment before beginning. "I think that I was seeing something that happened a long time ago. There was a cabin in the middle of the clearing. A cabin with no window glass. There was a woman not much older than Rosamar and I."

Ashley paused. She didn't want to remember the rest of it.

"When we were all in the clearing, you said something about there being a baby, too," Lucas said.

"Her name was Elizabeth," Ashley whispered.

Lucas waited, his hands on her shoulders. "There's more, isn't there?" he asked.

Ashley nodded. "That same man that I saw in the nursery was there, if he's even a man," she said. "Lucas, I know that this sounds crazy, but could there really be demons that live for hundreds of years?"

"Demons," Clay repeated. He picked up a stone and tossed it to the creek bed, where it landed with a muffled thump in the deep layer of leaves. "That dam needs to be rebuilt," he said. "Water's starting to seep through at the bottom."

Lucas looked at Clay, then back to Ashley. "What happened to the baby, Ash?" he asked.

"He killed her."

Clay threw another stone. "You were imagining

it. Sleeping on your feet," he said. "Nothing you saw was real. Not the cabin. Not the demon-man or whatever it is you think he is. And not the woman or her baby. It never happened."

Ashley looked at him and then down at the ground. She pulled away from Lucas and went to stand a few feet away, with her back to the others. She didn't want to see their expressions.

"Wait a minute," Rosamar said, after a long silence. "I just thought of something. Why would a hydrangea be growing out in the middle of the woods? They don't grow wild, do they?"

Lucas was the one that answered her. "Not that I know of," he said.

"It didn't grow wild," Ashley said, turning back. "Whoever built the cabin planted it there. The cabin stood right behind the spot where the hydrangea is now."

"Wouldn't it be easy to check whether or not there used to be a cabin there?" Rosamar said, turning to Clay. "Couldn't we go to the courthouse and find property records or something?"

"For what year? Eighteen-sixty? Nineteen hundred?" he asked. "Besides, I don't know if property records are going to show where a cabin was located. Maybe they just list the owner of the property and not what's been built on it. Do you know, Lucas?"

"We don't need to do all that," Lucas said. "If there was a cabin there once, then we should be able to find some sign of it in the clearing. Maybe the board they used for a threshold. Or part of the fireplace."

"Let's go," Rosamar said, slapping a mosquito and then wiping a smear of blood from her shin.

"There's no use arguing about whether or not the cabin existed. Let's just check it out."

Ashley looked at her. "I don't want to go back there ever again," she said. "You don't know what I saw."

Lucas took her hand. "It's too late to go this evening, anyway," he said. "It would get too dark too soon. We wouldn't be able to find anything."

His hand was warm, his palms callused from outdoor work. The bones of his hands were sturdy. For just a moment, Ashley had the sensation that she would be safe as long as she held onto his hand.

Then she looked past him to the dam and remembered all that she had seen and heard that day. The moss and the approaching night seemed to have softened the stones so that they had lost their definition, but she remembered how rough-edged they had looked earlier.

A night bird began singing somewhere near them, its voice loud and piercing. Ashley tensed, the shrill tone reminding her of the woman's screams. She turned back toward Lucas, putting her ear against his chest, covering her other ear with her hand.

Vernettie had accused her of suppressing the images that came to her, and she had been right, but Ashley knew now that there were some things that she could never forget.

EIGHT

That night Ashley dreamed of Vernettie's grand-mother for the first time.

Ashley stood at the creek, looking down at the bed on the dry side of the dam. An old woman with Vernettie's pale blue eyes, wispy yellow-blond hair, and erect posture—but with a different jawline—stood directly across from Ashley.

"Are you Grandmother Birdie?" Ashley asked.

The old woman nodded.

A feeling of breathless damp heat and darkness washed up from the creek bed, as if Ashley and the old woman stood on the brink of an abyss that might suck them both into its depths.

Then, not far from Grandmother Birdie, the demon rose from a crouch, his sunken eyes glittering. Ashley started to call out a warning, but then she saw something that thickened her voice in her throat.

Snakes writhed round his feet in tangled bunches.

Ashley tried to warn Grandmother Birdie, but she couldn't speak. Seemingly unaware of the danger that threatened her, the old woman bent forward from the waist as Ashley sometimes saw Vernettie do at the end of a long day, her fists bunched at the small of her back as if she were trying to ease the muscles there.

The demon lifted his withered arm. As if in obedience to his gesture, the snakes roiled, blunt heads and sinewy bodies emerging from the tangle as they slithered one by one toward Grandmother Birdie.

"Snakes," Ashley finally managed to say in a voice that sounded like a croak. "He can control the snakes."

Her warning was too late. Grandmother Birdie turned just as the snakes reached her, boiling over her black, thick-soled shoes. Ashley's hands flew to her throat as she watched.

Grandmother Birdie faced Ashley again, her gaze laden with a terrible intensity.

"How can I help you?" Ashley whispered.

With the snakes twisting round her ankles, the old woman lifted her arm, pointing down at the dry creek bed. "Hear this," she said. Her voice was high and quivery. Ashley strained to hear. "And your covenant with death shall be disannulled, and your agreement with hell shall not stand; when the overflowing scourge shall pass through, then ye shall be trodden down by it."

Snakes ringed Grandmother Birdie's calves. Panic caught at Ashley's breath, tightening her throat and her chest. "What does it mean?" she screamed. "Don't speak in riddles! Just tell me."

The dream seemed to stutter. Time passed without Ashley being aware of its passing. With horror, she saw that one of the snakes had wrapped itself around Grandmother Birdie's neck. The blunt-nosed head lay across her lips, silencing her. Her eyes were wide, the pupils ringed by white.

Ashley clawed at her own throat. She felt as if she were inside Grandmother Birdie's body, feeling that muscular length tightening around her neck, the scaly head sealing her own lips. She gasped, drawing in a great gulp of air. "What can I do?" she screamed again.

Grandmother Birdie did not speak, could not speak. It was up to Ashley to find the answer. She looked from Grandmother Birdie to the demon, and suddenly she understood something that she must have been meant to understand. If he could control the snakes, then he really must be something more than human. Or something less.

Ashley put her hands to her temples. What else had she been meant to learn from this dream? She had to learn everything, remember everything, and then she had to act on what she remembered.

Forcing herself to breathe deeply, she stared into Grandmother Birdie's eyes. "You said something about something being disannulled. Something about an agreement with hell, and something overflowing," she said, hoping for some confirming sign from Grandmother Birdie.

She didn't receive any. Instead, a pulsing contraction moved in waves along the length of the snake's body. Its upper body inched further up over Grandmother Birdie's chin, and its head angled so that its length lay along the direction of her lips, concealing them completely.

"No," Ashley screamed, stepping forward, swaying toward the edge of the bank and then regaining her balance. She glanced wildly about her, preparing to jump into the dry creek bed. She had to try something else, perhaps even try to pull the snake away from the old woman's throat and the others from around her feet. Ashley's fingertips tingled, as if she had already touched the cold muscles of the snakes.

Then she stopped, looked down at the bed of the creek. She looked at the dam to her right. "Overflow-

ing," she said. She met Grandmother Birdie's gaze and thought she saw an acknowledgment in her eyes.

"Water overflows," Ashley said. *"Is that it? Do we have to flood the creek?"*

The demon beat his chest with bony fists. The sound was horrible—like that of seeds rattling inside a dried gourd. He tore matted clumps of hair from his head. Heat and a putrid smell boiled across the dry creek toward Ashley, dragging up sand and bits of dried leaves with it. She screamed and backed away, a hand over her mouth.

"Look at me," Grandmother Birdie called.

Her chest heaving, Ashley turned back to Grandmother Birdie. She saw that the snake had fallen away from her neck, leaving red weals on the fragile skin. The other snakes slithered into the underbrush.

Grandmother Birdie laughed, lifting both arms above her head. Something in Ashley responded to her laughter. Joy rushed through her chest, as if the old woman's relief had emitted a spicy, fragrant odor that she had inhaled. She saw that the demon was gone. Seeing that, she laughed along with the old woman.

Ashley woke, still laughing under her breath.

Then fear pulled her lips back into a grimace.

The moonlight reflected off the swaying trees outside her window, casting a pattern of light on the wall above her bed. She lay still until her breathing eased, then turned over and pulled Nikki's bassinet closer to the edge of the bed. She put her hand on Nikki's back. Since convincing her parents to let her take over all of the night feedings, she had kept Nikki's bassinet in her room each night.

Nikki hiccupped in her sleep, her narrow back jerking under Ashley's fingers. Glancing at the clock,

Ashley saw that it was nearly three in the morning. Nikki should be waking any moment for her next bottle. Ashley made sure that none of her covers, or Nikki's, was hanging over the edge of the bed, and then lay back on her pillow.

The frames of her bed and of Nikki's bassinet were brass, too slick for a snake to climb. At least that was what she told herself as she lay still, waiting for her younger sister to stir.

Ashley didn't know that she had fallen asleep again until Nikki made a mewing sound, waking her. Ashley blinked in the strong sunlight, then sat up, brushing her hair out of her face.

Vernettie stood in the doorway, watching her.

"I dreamed last night," Ashley said.

Crossing the room, Vernettie picked up Ashley's journal from the bedside table. She took a pen out of the pocket of her skirt and handed both to Ashley. "Write down everything you remember," she said, bending over Nikki to check her diaper. "Do it first thing when you wake up every morning."

Ashley glanced at Vernettie, and then down at the journal. She spread her fingers across the suede cover. Inside this journal, she had recorded her feelings about Lucas, her hopes for a career as a journalist, her occasional anger with both her parents for spending so much time at the law firm that they had formed.

"Do you know who I saw in my dream?" Ashley asked.

Vernettie straightened, a hand on her lower back. She tilted her head to the side, looking down at Ashley. "No, how would I know?"

"Someone that looked like you, except that her chin was pointed and she was shorter."

For a moment, Vernettie said nothing, only looking into Ashley's eyes. Then the harsh lines from Vernettie's nose to the corners of her lips seemed to soften, and she almost smiled. "You must have seen Grandmother Birdie," she said. Then she did smile, the skin around her pale blue eyes crinkling. "I always hoped she'd come to me in my dreams. Her coming to you instead is almost as good."

Vernettie scooped up Nikki and headed toward the bathroom that connected Ashley's room and the nursery. "Write it down. Everything she said and did."

"I don't have to write it down," Ashley said. "I remember it all. And I found out something I didn't know. Yesterday, *he* sent that snake after me. He was trying to kill me so that he could get to Nikki."

At the doorway, Vernettie paused, turning to look at Ashley over her shoulder. "My grandmother told me that the dream-knowledge sometimes came to her in signs. Write it all down. Every detail. We'll study over it some when you finish."

Vernettie carried Nikki through into the other room. Ashley heard a drawer being opened and the jingling of the mobile over Nikki's crib. She listened for a moment, then she opened the journal and began writing.

When she finished, she stared at what she had written, remembering her laughter at three in the morning. Now, looking at the words, she felt a pressure at the back of her throat, and then a rush of blood to her face. Vernettie had been right to make her write down every detail, because in her horror-stricken fascination with the demon's command of the snakes, she had nearly forgotten the most important part of the dream: the part about flooding the dam.

She climbed out of bed, careful to hold the journal open, and went through into the nursery. She stood in the connecting doorway until Vernettie noticed her there and looked up. Vernettie had just finished changing Nikki's diaper.

Ashley held out the journal.

Vernettie came over, took it from her and then read the entry. She looked up at Ashley, her face expressionless.

Suddenly the constriction in Ashley's throat loosened and she could talk. "It's there, isn't it? How to stop him."

"I recognize the quotation," Vernettie said. "It's from the Old Testament. It's a prophecy."

Ashley grinned. "Well, it's a prophecy that we're going to put to good use."

Vernettie laid a cautioning hand on Ashley's arm. "We don't understand yet just what this means. Why would flooding the creek stop him? This is too important for you to go off half-cocked, Ashley Morgan."

"I'm not," she said. "I saw what happened to the demon when I realized what Grandmother Birdie was trying to tell me. He was scared. He didn't want me to know about the dam. We can't ignore what I learned or wait around for other signs. We have to do something now. Today."

Vernettie continued to look at her, but Ashley smiled a wide smile to convince her. "I'm sure about what I saw, Vernettie," she said. "I'm sure."

She felt a fluttering of something near the pit of her stomach, but she pushed the sensation away. She *was* sure. For Nikki's sake, she couldn't afford not to be.

NINE

Four hours later, Ashley stood at the front door, pretending a nonchalance she didn't feel as she said goodbye to her father. "If that other fax comes in," he said, "just . . ."

"Call Nelda at the office," Ashley said, finishing his sentence. She scanned the woods. For the last hour, the back of her neck had prickled whenever she had gone near a window. The euphoria that she had felt earlier had dissipated and had been replaced by this nagging worry. Standing outside, she felt even more exposed and vulnerable than she had inside the house.

Lucas and Clay were working in a flower bed near the curve in the driveway, taking out the plants that had wilted in the summer's heat. Lucas stood, shading his eyes as he looked in Ashley's direction.

"Dad, maybe you ought to take Nikki in to the office with you today," she said.

Her father shifted his briefcase to his other hand. "Is the babysitting getting to be too much for you?"

Ashley shook her head. "It's not that," she said, glancing into the woods. She looked back at her father, meeting his gaze. "It's just that I have that creepy feeling again that someone's out there in the woods."

Her father studied the woods, and then turned back

to Ashley. "There's no one there, Ash," he said. "There never was. It was all just a hallucination." His brows were bunched together, and he looked at her steadily. The sunlight caught his blond lashes, making them sparkle. She looked into her father's eyes for a long moment. Seeing the worry lines that fanned out from the corners of his eyes, she understood that the more she told him, the more he would doubt her.

She forced herself to smile, then shrug. "I guess that it'll just take me a little time to get over it."

Her father nodded, but he didn't appear convinced. His eyebrows didn't smooth, and his mouth still looked tensed.

"You'd better go," she said, patting him on the arm. "Mom's called three times to see why you haven't left yet."

He turned, his heels making hollow thunks against the flagstone walkway. He looked out across the property, then up at the square of sky visible above the house. "You know, I feel kind of jumpy myself," he said. "Maybe the weather's about to change."

Or maybe, Ashley thought, he had enough of the dreamer about him to be affected by what was happening without understanding why. She looked at the back of his head as he continued to study the sky. He had a cowlick that could never be completely controlled, no matter how expensive his haircut. She had the same cowlick and so did Nikki. It was a link among the three of them. Thinking about it made Ashley wonder whether Nikki might be aware of danger, beyond the usual sensitivity of babies to a tense atmosphere.

"Go on," Ashley said to her father, her voice soft. "Vernettie and I will take care of everything."

He turned, smiling. "You've done a good job helping Vernettie since your mother went back to work, but it's a lot of responsibility for a girl your age. I haven't really been keeping up with your activities, either. How's that correspondence course coming along?"

"To tell you the truth, Dad, I haven't worked on it much." She studied the woods once more, then looked back at him.

He pushed his hand through his hair, then shrugged. "I thought you needed to finish it this summer so that you would have room in your schedule for an extra year of science."

"I did, but I've decided that I don't want an extra credit in science. I was only doing that because you and Mom wanted me to."

"Because we wanted you to? I thought you liked science. You make such good grades in it."

It was Ashley's turn to shrug. "I study a lot," she said. "And I do like it some. Because there's always a solution to every problem. I just don't like it enough to give up the other things I want to study."

"Isn't it too late to drop the correspondence course?" her father asked. "For that matter, haven't you already registered for Biology II?"

"I'll call my counselor," she said. "And I'll pay you back for the course."

"You bet you will," her father said, smiling. He checked his watch, then said, "Well, let's talk about it when we have more time." He leaned toward her, kissing her on the forehead. Then he walked away, pulling his keys out of his pocket.

That was it: no anger, no pleading. She had imagined that there would be a worse scene when she finally got up the nerve to tell her parents that she had changed her mind about the correspondence course, but she could see now that she had been afraid for no reason.

After her father had driven away, Lucas crossed the asphalt toward Ashley, a trowel in his hand. Sweat ran in lines down either side of his face and neck. He had taken off his shirt. There was a smudge of dirt on his right side below his ribs. He wiped off his forehead with the back of his arm.

She looked at him and felt a dull heaviness gather in the center of her chest. Lucas hadn't called her the night before, hadn't whistled a hello when he arrived for work that morning, as he often did. Maybe everything that he had witnessed yesterday had changed his feelings about her. She wouldn't blame him, but she had counted on Lucas sticking with her.

He leaned forward, kissing her forehead. He was careful to hold the trowel away from her. "You okay this morning?" he asked.

Ashley nodded. "Pretty good," she said, watching his expression for signs of contempt or pity.

"I've got something to tell you," he said.

"I don't think I want to hear it," she said, but then she made up her mind to stop hiding from things she didn't want to know. "No, tell me," she said.

Transferring the trowel from his right hand to his left, Lucas touched Ashley's arm. "I think you'll want to hear this," he said. "Clay and I rode in early with Vernettie this morning. We went back to the clearing."

Ashley looked across to Clay. He was filling a wheelbarrow with the wilted plants. He seemed to feel her gaze on him. He turned to look at her.

"We found what looks like a foundation for a chimney," Lucas said.

Looking back at him, Ashley said, "So there was

78

a cabin there after all.'' She was glad that she hadn't eaten breakfast, because suddenly her stomach did a flipflop. Her eyes watered. "And everything that I saw yesterday could actually have happened some time in the past." She lowered her voice to a whisper. "I think that I would have rather found out that I really was hallucinating."

Lucas pitched the trowel off to the side and took both her hands in his. "I knew that you didn't want to go back there, but I thought you'd want to know for sure. And the rest of us needed to know."

Ashley leaned toward him, letting her forehead rest against his bare shoulder. She was too miserable to say anything for a moment, but then she sighed and straightened again. She looked across to where Clay had been, but he and the wheelbarrow were gone. Glancing farther up the drive, she saw him wheeling the dead plants toward the composter. His shoulders were down and he was moving quickly. She smiled. "Clay doesn't look too happy about being proven wrong," she said.

Lucas glanced at him. "He's still trying to convince himself that it doesn't mean anything," he said.

"And you?" Ashley asked. "Are you trying to convince yourself that it doesn't mean anything, too?"

"I'm going to be honest with you," he said. "I believed you enough to go looking for proof that the cabin was there, and I've believed all along that you really did see someone in Nikki's room, but I don't know how much of the rest of it I can handle."

"Me, either," Ashley said. "I'm the one that saw it and I don't know how much else I can handle."

Lucas released her hands. With the back of his hand, he touched her cheek. "So what do we do now?'' he asked, bending down to retrieve the trowel.

Watching him, Ashley said, ''I have a question about something Clay said yesterday. He said that the dam needed some work. What will happen if the dam's not repaired?''

Lucas's eyebrow went up, but he said, ''Nothing much will happen for a while even if we don't repair it. Eventually it would weaken to the point that it would fall. Probably during a rainstorm. And then no one will be able to get a car in or out until it's rebuilt.''

Ashley looked down the drive and then at him.

With the trowel, he gestured toward the point where the driveway dipped, following the curve of the land. ''Before the dam was built, there were two arms to the creek,'' he said. ''They used to split and then meet again somewhere below there.''

Ashley thought about what he was describing. She pictured the land, the creek that already curved around three sides of their property. ''Without the dam, the creek would totally surround the property?'' she asked.

''Like a moat around a castle,'' Lucas answered, turning back to her. He smiled.

Like a moat around a castle.

Suddenly Ashley felt as if she had received the confirmation that she had wanted in the dream. If the demon were for some reason afraid of water, and the rise on which the house stood would be surrounded by water, then he couldn't get near Nikki.

She laughed in surprise at the simplicity of the solution, then laughed harder at the puzzled expression on Lucas's face.

TEN

Relief lightened the heaviness in Ashley's chest. She felt as if her bones were growing more porous and her lungs deeper, so that she might breathe in enormous quantities of the air that was scented with honeysuckle and jasmine. Solving this problem was going to be easier than she had thought. "The dam must have been completed just before Elizabeth was killed," she told Lucas. "That's why there were still dead fish on the bed of the creek when I ran away from the cabin."

"What dead fish?" Lucas asked, but then he turned at the sound of a car horn beeping. "It's Rosie," he said.

Just then Vernettie walked outside, looked down the drive, and then joined them on the flagstone walk to wait for Rosamar. Vernettie held Nikki facing forward, with Nikki's back snuggled against her thin chest.

When Nikki spotted Ashley, her feet cycled and her whole body wiggled. Lucas reached out, catching one of Nikki's bare feet in mid-cycle, then he laughed at the surprised expression on her face. "Her skin is so soft," he said. "Like a marshmallow."

"After she starts walking, the bottoms of her feet will toughen up quick enough," Vernettie said.

Ashley turned away, waiting as Rosamar parked

the car under the shade of a live oak. Suddenly she didn't feel so certain about her conclusions. If she had guessed wrong about what the dream meant, then Nikki might never get her chance to walk.

When Rosamar got out of the car, she asked her brother, "Did you find anything?"

Nodding, Lucas said, "Part of a chimney."

"I knew it," Rosamar said. Her grin was a lopsided version of her usual wide smile. She started toward Ashley and Lucas, but then stopped and turned around, looking off into the woods.

Doubt collapsed what was left of Ashley's good mood. Even Rosamar sensed the brooding, malignant atmosphere out there.

Clay walked up just as Rosamar turned back. He took off his baseball cap. After wiping his face on the back of his arm, he ran his hand through his blond hair, making it stand on end rather than smoothing it as he must have intended. When he lowered his arm, his elbow bumped Rosamar's shoulder.

Rosamar looked up at him, smiling. The effect on Clay was immediate, and one that Ashley wouldn't have anticipated. Red crept up from his neck, flushing his face.

Rosamar grinned, obviously noticing his discomfort and pleased by it.

Lucas turned away from Nikki. "Ashley was just telling me something about the dam," he said to the others.

Ashley's confidence in her interpretation of the dream had eroded in the moments since Rosamar had arrived. Under Clay's scrutiny, her voice faltered as she repeated what she had told Lucas, then filled in details from her dream. "If the dam was finished only a couple of days before Elizabeth was killed, as

I'm pretty sure it was, then that might mean that the demon couldn't get to her before then,'' she said, glancing toward the woods.

Clay made a sound under his breath. Ashley stopped, realizing by Clay's reaction that she had said the word *demon* out loud again, something she hadn't meant to do after his reaction the last time. She hesitated, feeling her face flush, but then she went on. "We can flood the creek by knocking down the dam," she said. "Then, if Lucas is right, the whole property will be surrounded by water. That might be enough to protect Nikki.''

Clay shifted his feet, the leather soles of his boots grating against the light coating of the sand that had blown across the asphalt. "I can't go along with that," he said. "Finding the foundation of a chimney this morning sure as heck doesn't mean that all that other stuff happened. You probably heard about that cabin somewhere and then forgot all about it until yesterday when it got mixed up in your mind with the rest of that stuff you've been worried about.''

Lucas started to say something, but Rosamar broke in. "You have a hard time believing in anything, don't you?'' she asked Clay. She was so much shorter than he was that she had to arch her neck back to see his face.

"I like to be logical,'' Clay said. "And most of this just doesn't make sense.''

"Sometimes things don't make sense,'' Rosamar said. "Sometimes you have to trust your gut feelings.''

"I notice that's mostly what you do,'' Clay said. "If I remember correctly, trusting your gut feelings was the main reason we ended up helping Ashley search the woods, and look how that turned out!''

Lucas's crooked eyebrow rose. Ashley thought she saw a quick smile cross his lips.

"I'm helping with the dam, whether you do or not," Rosamar said. Her fisted hands were on her hips.

"No insult intended, but your help's not going to matter much one way or another. You and Ashley don't know a thing about dismantling a dam."

"Neither do you."

"I'm majoring in architecture at the university," Clay said. "I know a bit more about structural engineering than you do." He glanced at his grandmother, then put his cap on again.

"You just finished your first year in college," Rosamar said. "You probably studied calculus and first year physics, like Lucas did. You don't know any more about dams than I do." She tossed her head, so that her hair swung back away from her face.

Lucas laughed. "She's got you there," he said.

Clay's face flushed a fierce red. He closed his mouth and tilted his head back, looking up at the sky.

"And, after our discussion with Ashley's father this morning, I'm surprised to hear that you won't be helping Ashley and Rosie work on the dam," Lucas told Clay. Turning to Ashley, he said, "You didn't give me a chance to finish telling you about the dam when you were asking me questions earlier. Clay and I were talking to your father just this morning about the seepage we saw yesterday. He's already okayed the extra hours to rebuild the dam."

"To rebuild it," Clay said. "Not to take it down completely. The whole idea was to keep the dam from being washed away the next big rain we have. Mr. and Mrs. Morgan are not going to take kindly to having their driveway flooded and not being able to get their cars in or out of the garage. Or did you think they wouldn't notice?"

Lucas looked at Ashley. "He's right," he said.

"I know," Ashley answered, "but it's the only idea that I have right now. Can we take out enough stones to flood the creek temporarily, and then we'll figure out what to do from there?"

Raising his eyebrows, Lucas looked at Clay. "How about it? Sounds like a good compromise to me. We were going to take some of those stones out anyway in order to repair the dam."

In answer, Clay shrugged.

"And we can start right away?" Ashley asked.

Clay turned away, flinging his long arms out. He muttered something that Ashley couldn't hear, then let his arms fall.

Still watching Clay, Lucas shook his head. "First thing tomorrow," he said. "We have work that your father expects us to get done today. Besides, we need some tools that we don't have, and Clay and I ought to go back to the dam and plan out the work. All that will take us most of the day."

"What are you going to do about this little one?" Vernettie asked.

Ashley looked across the drive and into the woods. "I don't know," she said. "We can't risk leaving you and her alone here."

Clay spoke. "I absolutely refuse to bring her with us to work on the dam," he said. "It's too hot out there for a baby and we'll be working too hard to watch her closely enough."

Shaking her head, Ashley said, "I wasn't going to suggest that. I don't want her in the woods, either." She looked at Vernettie. "You'll have to take her away somewhere. To your house, maybe. That should be far enough away.''

"Your parents might try to call," Vernettie said. "They don't want me trooping all over town with her."

"Take the cellular phone. Transfer all the calls to that line. They don't have to know that you're not at home."

"You're going to end up getting yourself fired, Grandma," Clay said. He turned and stomped off toward the storage building behind the house.

Rosamar watched him, but she seemed more amused than put off by his reaction. Smiling, she turned and faced Ashley. "I've got an open workout at gymnastics in an hour," she said. "Why don't you come watch and then we can go out to lunch together? It's been a long time since we've done anything fun together."

Shaking her head, Ashley said, "I don't want to leave Nikki."

Rosamar walked past her, holding out her arms for the baby. "We're taking her with us, of course," she said.

While Rosamar worked on a new dismount on parallel bars suspended above a foam-filled pit, Ashley and Nikki shared a crowded bench with the mothers of the younger gymnasts. Nikki drew attention from many of the women. Ashley enjoyed showing her off. She wished that this were all there were to being a big sister, but for her it carried a responsibility that these women could not envision.

Once the interest in Nikki died down, Ashley tried to pay attention to Rosamar's practice session. Rosamar would want to know how her new trick had looked. Ashley's thoughts kept returning to her dream and the plans to dismantle the dam. There had to be a reason why the flowing stream might keep the demon away from Nikki, some *logical* reason, as Clay might put it, but Ashley couldn't think of one.

She was glad when Rosamar cut her workout short. Rosamar dressed quickly, and then they drove to the mall. After stopping so that Rosamar could buy a new CD, they headed for the soup and sandwich shop, with Ashley pushing Nikki's stroller.

"You and Lucas should be doing this," Rosamar said.

"Going to the mall?"

Rosamar shook her head. "Not to the mall, necessarily. Just going out."

Hearing a noise from Nikki, Ashley stopped and knelt down by the stroller. When Nikki saw her face, her eyes rounded. Ashley touched her cheek. "Has Lucas been complaining?" she asked.

"No," Rosamar said, "but he seems worried. He's a good guy, Ash. He deserves to have some fun every now and then. So do you."

Straightening, Ashley glanced at her. "I didn't want any of this to happen," she said, reaching for the handles on the stroller.

"Let me do it for a while," Rosamar said, taking the stroller. She bent forward, looking down at Nikki from between the handles. "Better buckle your safety helmet, kid," she warned.

"Stop!" Ashley said, so loudly that several shoppers walking ahead of them glanced back over their shoulders.

"She forgot to take her medicine today," Rosamar said, making a circle in front of her ear and then pointing to Ashley.

Laughing, the shoppers turned back and continued walking. Rosamar waited a moment, then started pushing the stroller. "Relax," she said. "You know that I wouldn't do anything to hurt Nikki."

Ashley fell into step beside her. "I know," she said. "You and Lucas have been great. Clay, too, despite all of his grumbling."

They continued walking, as Ashley thought about what Rosamar had said. "I do want to go out with Lucas," she said. "I miss all of the things that we used to do. But my parents don't believe that anyone was ever in our house trying to get Nikki. They would just put her to sleep in her nursery, alone, like any other baby."

Before going to bed that night, Ashley called Lucas. "Hi," she said, when he answered. "I just wanted you to know that I was thinking about you."

"Me, too," he said. "I was thinking about you, too."

Ashley sat on the edge of her bed and looked down at Nikki. "You know, later this summer, after all of this is over, it might be fun to go to Astroworld," she said. "My treat. Maybe we could get Rosamar and Clay to go with us."

"Or maybe we could just go alone," Lucas said. "I would like to be alone with you, Ashley."

Feeling both embarrassed and pleased, Ashley sat back against her headboard. She and Lucas talked only a few moments longer, but when she hung up the telephone, she felt more hopeful about her relationship with him than she had since the day that she had seen the demon in the nursery.

Maybe that was why it was such a surprise to dream about the young man again. When Ashley went to sleep, a three-quarters moon hung over the tops of the trees, but soon she was dreaming of a day in which the sunlight shone down on a horrifying scene.

The young man was being dragged through the empty village by a woman and a youth, survivors from a nearby village. The youth, walking backward, grasped both of the young man's arms and the woman his legs. He tried to hold his head up, but the weakness was too great and he let it fall back. His long hair dragged through the debris along the path. Sometimes the back of his head bumped against the ground. Leggings protected his hips from being scraped, but dirt and bits of leaves were embedded in the torn places on his back. He had long since stopped screaming. Now he saved his strength for breathing.

They followed the slow progress of the one-armed man and his companion. After darting a fearful glance at the one-armed man, the youth let the young man's upper body fall to the ground. Before the young man could draw another painful breath, the youth leaned over him and whispered, "Die, Charnas. Die quickly. It is your time. Do not fight it any longer. For your sake and ours."

"I cannot," Charnas gasped. "When I die, the last of my line dies."

The woman whispered something to the youth and motioned to him. The one-armed man stopped. With a hurried glance over his shoulder, the youth scrambled to his feet and grabbed the arms of the young man again.

When Ashley woke the next morning, anxiety had settled beneath her heart. She tried to put the young man named Charnas out of her mind, but a sense of doom stayed with her as she and the others gathered tools and supplies and headed into the woods.

ELEVEN

Thirty minutes after the group had started into the woods, Ashley stood beside Rosamar at the edge of the bank. Ashley clutched the branch that she had carried as a protection against snakes. She and Rosamar watched as Lucas and Clay walked back and forth along the top of the dam. Underneath the shade of a dogwood, a sledgehammer and pick leaned against a cooler which held their drinks and snacks.

Ashley's anxiety had deepened as they had neared the dam. Their trek through the woods had been uneventful, but now, looking at the dam, she was overcome with dismay. "It's so much bigger than I remembered," she said.

Lucas and Clay crouched near the center of the stone structure. The stones were flat and were set in distinct layers. "This is going to be a tough job," Lucas said, looking up. "Yesterday, when Clay and I tried prying up this stone, we found out that all the moisture and grit and algae has almost cemented the stones together."

Clay stood. "Except where it's leaking through down there," he said, pointing toward the bottom. He leaned forward.

Ashley looked away from the dam, along the

length of the dry bed of the creek, down to where it made a turn to the left, and then she looked into the woods on the other side of the bank.

"What is it?" Rosamar asked.

Ashley crossed her arms over her chest. "I don't know," she said, looking over at Rosamar and noticing how pale her friend appeared. "I was thinking about the lair Vernettie's grandmother told her about. Wondering where it would be."

Lucas strode to the bank, picking up the tools. Clay followed and took the sledgehammer from him. Neither Rosamar nor Ashley said anything about the lair while Clay was near. Ashley looked at the pines that stood back from the edge of the bank, at the brush that grew chest-high in places. "He could be hiding in there now, and we'd never see him," she said to Rosamar as soon as Lucas and Clay had moved back to the dam.

Rosamar grunted. "But we'd smell him, wouldn't we? If he smells as bad as you say?"

Ashley looked at her and then back at the brush. "Maybe not. He could be downwind of us." Saliva gathered in her mouth at the memory of his musk. She tightened her fingers around her branch.

"Time to get to work," Clay said.

They divided the work as evenly as possible, but when Ashley straightened sometime in the mid-afternoon and looked down at her hands, she winced. She had been feeling the blisters for the last hour, but she saw that three of her knuckles were also scraped and bloody. Two nails had broken off, one below the quick.

Lucas noticed. "Let's take a break," he called.

After waiting for the others to fill their cups and then gulping down her own share of the water, Ashley stretched out on her back·on the ground, her knees bent and her arms crossed behind her head. Patches of gunmetal-colored sky were visible through the breaks in the trees.

The day before, Clay and Lucas had decided on breaking out a V-shaped opening in the center of the dam, rather than taking off one whole layer of stones at a time. Clay wanted the dam repaired in the most efficient manner, and Ashley wanted the creek flooded as quickly as possible. The method seemed to fit both purposes. Now Ashley turned on her side and studied the pile of stones on the bank. "We're not making much progress, are we?" she asked.

Lucas had been sitting with his arms folded over his bent knees as he studied the dam. "The channel is narrowing too quickly," he said. "It'll come to a point before we get down to water level, unless we widen it from the top down." He stood up, walking back to the dam. Clay followed.

Rosamar was stretched out on the ground, with an arm thrown across her eyes. Ashley watched her for a moment, then looked at Lucas and Clay, and then at the brush along the opposite bank. She rotated her shoulders, trying to ease the soreness. The exhausting work, or the heat, or both, seemed to have driven away the miasma that had cloaked everything in the forest when they had first arrived at the dam. She no longer sensed a threat. The woods seemed, well, like woods. Nothing more.

Getting up, she walked to the bank, but instead of following Lucas and Clay onto the dam, she stood looking down at the water on the pond side. Near the stones, green algae filmed the surface, but farther out the water was clear and dark and still. Minnows darted near the bank and then away. A large water spider rested on the surface. Everything seemed peaceful and free of harm.

She turned, looking at the bed on the dry side of the dam. Close to the dam, it was floored with a swampy mixture of weeds, decaying leaves and mud. There were no dead fish, as there had been yesterday. She breathed in deeply. She smelled only the rank odor of the weeds, her own sweat, and a hot powdery smell that came from the stones they had dislodged. The breeze had died in the heat of the afternoon, so that the demon's musk would have drifted to them if he had been near.

"We won't get down to water level today, but we'll get close," Lucas said, joining her.

She turned, resting her forehead against his shoulder. She was too tired and sticky with sweat to hug him, but she smiled and then kissed his chin. The two of them had worked together all morning, carrying away the stones that Clay and Rosamar dislodged. Every time they carried a stone to the bank, one or the other of them had to walk backward, balancing awkwardly on the uneven surface of the dam. They had worked well together, instinctively and with little need for conversation.

"We're getting there," Clay said, adding his own encouragement. Surprisingly, as the day had progressed and the others had become increasingly dejected, Clay had become more cheerful. He had always been more happy with actions than with words, and he attacked the work as if he were in a rock-breaking contest and a championship were at stake. Ashley smiled at him, wondering if his spurt of enthusiasm had anything to do with a newly formed desire to impress Rosamar.

As Lucas and Clay moved to the dam again, Ashley scanned the woods once more. Nothing. She had no sense of the demon at all.

"Ready to get started again?" she asked, turning to look at Rosamar. Rosamar lifted her head, looking at her from under her shading arm.

"It's too cramped here for all of us to work at the same time," Lucas said. "Why don't you and Rosie rest for a while longer?"

Rosamar yawned. "Sounds good to me," she said, sitting up. She got up and rummaged through the picnic basket.

"We should do our part, too," Ashley said, but when Lucas climbed down into the cramped, V-shaped space without answering, she didn't repeat her protest. Now that she had stopped working, her arms and shoulders felt stiff. She looked at Rosamar, who shrugged and held out a bunch of red grapes. Ashley shook her head.

Clay swung the sledgehammer. Stone grated against stone. Some of the stones were easier to dislodge than others, and this one had come loose at the first blow. There was a muffled clunk as Clay dropped the sledgehammer behind him, on the unbroken surface of the dam. Clay bent to help Lucas lift the stone.

The grating stones reminded Ashley of bone rubbing against bone. She studied the bed of the creek for as far as she could see, looking for changes in contour. She looked across, at the opposite bank.

Maybe now, when she was too tired to be afraid but not sleepy enough to be vulnerable to the dreams, she should try to find the lair.

Lucas and Clay maneuvered the newly dislodged stone up the rough steps created by their staggered removal of the other layers, then walked it out to the bank. Ashley stepped aside to let them pass. She listened to their grunted instructions to each other, then looked up to watch a cardinal flit through the shade underneath the trees on the opposite bank. If the demon had killed Elizabeth only after the dam had been completed, it seemed likely to her that his lair was over there. Elizabeth had been much older than Nikki, perhaps six or seven months old. She didn't think that the demon would have willingly waited that long to attack her. He must have been held back by the water.

Lucas and Clay dropped the stone onto the pile on the bank. Ashley picked up the branch that she had carried through the woods earlier, then started across the dam, careful of her footing on the different levels. She stepped over the sledgehammer that Clay had left behind. On the other side of the bank, she took a step forward, heard a twig snap under her feet, and then kept going.

She was three or four yards away from the bank when Rosamar caught up. "You're going to find his lair, aren't you?" she asked.

Ashley stopped long enough to peer into the dense growth that began only a few yards away, testing her senses. She felt a need to be cautious, but not the floating anxiety that had nagged her that morning. "Yes," she said.

Just then, Lucas called out to her. She turned, her hands loose at her side. "It's okay," she told him. "You and Clay go on working. He's not out there."

"How do you know?" Rosamar asked. She pursed her lips as she bent forward, looking closely at the foliage just in front of them.

Ashley shook her head. "I can't tell you that," she said. "All I can tell you is that he's not out there."

She started off.

"Then where is he?" Rosamar asked.

Ashley didn't have an answer.

Ashley trudged through an area of the woods where the spreading shade of hardwoods crowded out the clean-smelling pines. Rosamar followed, ranging off to the side to investigate a bowl-shaped depression, then angling back to meet up with Ashley as they passed into a clearing. The sun's heat had burned some of the moisture from the air, but still sweat ran in a line down the middle of her back, soaking the waistband of her shorts. Her breathing was as ragged as if she were climbing a steep incline, rather than moving across relatively level terrain.

Rosamar touched Ashley's elbow. "You're winded," she said. "Let's rest here."

Nodding, Ashley stopped. A bird took wing above them, his movements accompanied by a hectic rustling of leaves. The air carried a faint scent of blackberries growing on a hedge not far away.

Rosamar plopped down on the ground, then lifted up to look underneath her bottom. "I forgot to check for poison ivy," she said, when she saw Ashley looking at her.

"And snakes," Ashley said. She turned in a circle, looking closely at the ground, but saw nothing. Dropping the branch, she sat, putting her hand to the ground to steady herself. Pain seared her shoulder. "Ow!" she cried.

"I know," Rosamar said, massaging her own shoulder. "Good thing that I don't have a meet coming up. I'm afraid my bars routine wouldn't measure up."

Ashley tried to settle herself, first leaning forward

with her hands wrapped around her knees, then sitting back propped against a tree, but neither position was comfortable. Her shoulders felt as if they had been dislocated. Even her hips and thighs were sore from the strain of lifting the heavy rocks. "There's no use trying to rest," she said, standing up again. She suddenly felt desperately tired.

Through a gap in the trees, she could make out another clearing fifty or sixty yards away. The ground rose to a small prominence in the center. Leaves had dropped along the perimeter, tattering the edges, but no vegetation grew within the clearing itself.

Ashley's eyes were itchy, her eyesight blurred. By some trick of the light, the clearing appeared darker than the surrounding woods. She turned, sighing, and found that Rosamar was watching her intently, her eyebrows drawn together.

"I'm fine, I'm okay," Ashley said, trying to smile as she glanced back. "Do you see that purply-black looking fungus over there?" she asked. "It's covering the whole clearing." The surface of the fungus appeared to have cracked, exposing the soil beneath it in light-colored veins.

"Who wants to look at fungus?" Rosamar said. She eased her legs out straight.

The cracks widened near the prominence. The veins ran like magma from the highest point. It was as if the earth had heaved itself up and broken the crust that had covered it. Ashley tried to imagine a geological process that might have produced what she was seeing.

A breeze started somewhere off in the woods, the sound rising and moving toward them. The wind whirled up a dirt devil that danced around the prominence, gathering up bits and pieces of fungi and sand and leaves before it whirled itself away. Fascinated, Ashley watched.

"What are you staring at?" Rosamar asked. Then, as if her own words or Ashley's absorption had frightened her, she scrambled to her feet and turned.

The two girls faced into a breeze that had already traveled over the prominence, dipping among the scattered leaves, the black fungus, the grains of sandy soil. Ashley breathed in deeply, taking in these scents.

And another, carried to her in faint molecules of musk and urine and rot. She straightened, jolted into alertness.

"Is that it?" Rosamar asked.

"That's his musk," Ashley whispered. "So it must be his lair."

Ashley started toward the clearing, and a thin, bony finger wrapped itself around her ankle.

She leaped forward, voiceless with terror, tugging against what turned out to be a bramble tangled in her sock. The bramble dug deeper, piercing through sock and skin to draw bright red blood. Rosamar ran to her, kneeling and holding her upraised leg still with one hand while she untangled the vine with the other. The muscles in Ashley's supporting leg quivered.

Rosamar remained kneeling, looking up, but for a moment Ashley couldn't speak. Her heart seemed to rise high in her chest, beating against her ribs. She forced herself to breathe deeply, evenly, until she regained her voice. "I thought it was him," she whispered. "Or a snake."

Rising straight from her squatting position, Rosamar said, "Maybe we ought to go back for the guys. We might need help."

"I thought that you weren't sure you believed in this," Ashley said.

Rosamar turned, facing the prominence, then looked at Ashley. "It's like I told Clay. None of this makes any sense."

"No, it doesn't," Ashley answered.

The two girls looked at each other through a long moment. Rosamar's face looked almost wiped clean of emotion, but Ashley knew her every expression, and she knew that Rosamar was struggling with indecision and, maybe, fear. "You said before that you didn't think he was in the woods now," Rosamar said. "Have you changed your mind? Does it feel like he's there now?"

"No, I haven't changed my mind," Ashley said. "We have to watch out for snakes, but not for him, I don't think." She started out again, veering to the left, skirting the edge of the clearing. Rosamar followed. Ashley's skin felt hot and prickly with sweat. Her hair clung to the back of her neck and the sides of her face.

Suddenly her nostrils widened. She smelled the demon's musk, strong and pungent.

"He's here," Rosamar said, backing up a step.

"No. I don't think so," Ashley said. She sensed an emptiness, a void that went beyond the lack of insect or bird life that might have been expected to inhabit the clearing. The demon was gone, and had been for some time.

The fungus that had appeared a single, flat shade of purply-black from a distance now revealed itself as a cracked maze of wet purple and reddish black. Fissures extended several inches into the soil. Ashley swallowed, inching forward.

"Oh, no," Rosamar moaned, pointing upward.

Ashley looked where she was pointing. Bagworms

infested the trees that ringed the clearing. Gosamer bags of crawling insects hung from leafless limbs. "That's why the clearing is so dark," Ashley said. The sunlight was diluted by the cocoon-like fabric of the bags.

"Let's get out of here," Rosamar said.

"No," Ashley said, crouching as she moved forward again. "This might be our only chance to get this close."

They tried not to step on the fallen branches as they moved. Instead of snapping cleanly, the branches compressed into dried powder underfoot. Bark had fallen from some of the trees. A thick sap oozed from the lesions.

"I'm afraid to breathe," Rosamar said.

"How do you think he gets in and out?" Ashley whispered, as she eased around. The prominence bulged to one side.

The strange half-light cast everything into shadow. Creeping forward, Ashley was about to step down when Rosamar suddenly shouted, "Watch out!"

Surprised by Rosamar's shout, Ashley stumbled. Trying to recover her footing, she placed her foot awkwardly. She staggered forward, unable to regain her balance.

A tree seemed to rush toward her. She twisted to the right to avoid slamming into the trunk.

She landed on the ground. Her forearms hit first, jarring her elbows and her shoulders. Nerves screamed in her shoulders and neck.

Rosamar knelt next to her. "Are you hurt?" she asked, touching Ashley's back.

"I don't think so," Ashley said, her voice wheezing.

"You were under the bagworms," Rosamar said. "That's why I yelled." She looked over her shoulder. "Hurry and get up," she said. "We're both under them now."

Strands of Ashley's hair dragged along the scummy surface of the soil when she moved her head. With thumb and forefinger, Rosamar lifted the strands free of the muck. Coughing, Ashley got to her hands and knees, then sat back against her heels, looking down at her clothing. A bitter, mildewy sourness was ground into her T-shirt and shorts. She wiped her hands on the back of her shorts as she looked at the prominence.

If she hadn't fallen, they might never have discovered the opening. Powdery dust dislodged by her fall sifted down, forming a concavity along one side of the bulge. Someone, the demon probably, had silted over the opening with a thin layer of baked mud.

"Do you see that?" she asked.

Bracing her hands on her thighs, Rosamar leaned forward. "That can't be the way he gets in and out. The opening is too small."

Ashley sat still for a moment, studying the cupped place in the soil. If she broke away the thin layer of dried mud that remained, the opening would measure only six to eight inches in diameter.

She remembered the sound of bone scraping against bone as he walked. Her esophagus burned as a bitter taste rose in her throat. "He doesn't have much flesh," she said. "I don't think his bones are connected to each other right, either. He could probably fit."

She thought of him rising, pushing up the layers of earth that buried him.

Or perhaps his decaying body gave off gases that finally erupted from the earth and opened a way for him.

"Do you think that he knows when there's a baby for him?" Rosamar asked, as if her thoughts were moving along the same line as Ashley's.

"I don't know," Ashley said, standing up. Rosamar's mention of a baby had triggered something, an involuntary spasm of fear.

"Maybe he comes up at certain time intervals whether there's a baby for him or not," Rosamar said, getting to her feet. "Maybe he has to go look for one."

Ashley turned, scanning the woods. When she moved, her own smell drifted up to her nostrils. She smelled of the demon's musk, as if she had assumed a share in his evil. She turned again.

Nothing. She still didn't sense him watching her, as she had earlier that day. Suddenly it seemed important to know how long it had been since she had felt him watching her.

"What's wrong?" Rosamar asked.

Ashley swallowed the saliva that had gathered in her mouth. "I don't know," she said, not bothering to whisper this time. All of the hours that she and the others had been away from the house replayed themselves one by one in her mind.

She realized what was bothering her.

There would be only one reason for the demon to have left the woods.

Vernettie must have returned to the house. The demon had gone there to find Nikki.

TWELVE

Ashley started for home.

"Wait," Rosamar cried, running after her. She caught up, grabbing the back of Ashley's T-shirt. "Should I get Lucas and Clay?"

Ashley tugged her shirt out of Rosamar's grasp. "Yes, get them," she shouted.

She glanced back, noted Rosamar's pale, clammy skin, and stopped again. "You'll be okay," she said. "The demon isn't out here. I think that he's somewhere near the house."

Ashley and Rosamar had angled far to the northeast of the dam while searching for the lair. Rosamar headed back toward the dam, but Ashley cut straight toward the house, intending to save time by crossing the creek above the dam. As the sounds of Rosamar's passage receded, she realized how comforting they had been and how alone she felt now.

As she ran, she glanced up at the sky, trying to gauge the time. She didn't think that it was time for her parents to come home—the only reason she could imagine for Vernettie to return—yet she was convinced that Vernettie had. A cloud of gnats accompanied her, seemingly anticipating her every shift in direction. She couldn't move fast enough to outrun them. Birds called out overhead, flitting from tree to tree whenever the noise of her clumsy passage through the woods disturbed them.

If the demon were waiting for her, then he would know that she was coming.

Her feet seemed too heavy to lift, but she pushed harder. Unlike Rosamar, she had never been particularly athletic. Breaking up the stones at the dam had sapped what little strength she had. Still, she broke through the trees much sooner than she expected, drawing up short at the edge of the bank.

She stood in front of the creek, not far from the point at which it emptied into the small pond created when the dam was built. She was probably at least a half-mile from Lucas and the others, she guessed. She paused, hands on her hips, staring down into the water. Trying to catch her breath, she lifted one foot at a time and then pressed down with her heel to ease the sudden cramping pain in her hamstrings.

The banks at this point were high and separated by a distance of almost fifteen feet—too wide a distance to leap—but the creek seemed to be only about five or six feet deep. Minnows darted through the clear, dark green of the water. Ashley smiled grimly, then bent down to pull off her shoes. It was this clean water, undammed, its purifying power unleashed, that would banish the demon.

Now that she had stopped running, pain seared her muscles and joints at each movement. Her movements were uncoordinated and clumsy, but she managed to toss her shoes one after the other onto the opposite bank. Then, holding her breath, she stepped off the bank, plunging into the water feet first, anticipating a jolt when her feet hit bottom.

There was no jolt. Underwater, Ashley's eyes

opened wide and her body went limp. The water level was much deeper than she had anticipated. The tepid water lapped at her, washing away the dried sweat, cleansing her. She floated for a moment, suspended, eyes half-closed. After she got over the initial surprise at its depth, she relaxed into the silence, feeling that it insulated her from the outside world. She was so tired. She let the gentle current turn her onto her right side.

Then the muscles at the backs of her thighs contracted viciously, drawing her legs up until her heels were near her bottom.

She opened her mouth to scream with the pain and, instead, gulped water.

Her thrashing churned up mud from the bottom of the creek. Dark flames of mud crawled upward through the water. She flailed her arms, desperate to get to the surface, but the muscles in her arms and shoulders seemed unstrung and those in her legs refused to release.

She was drowning.

No, she thought. That couldn't be true. She couldn't be drowning in the creek, so near her own house.

Her chest burned. The muscles in her legs clamped tighter, and hard pain filled her. She doubled over, grasping her knees with her arms. The dark flames touched her face and she tasted the rank sludge on her tongue.

She stopped fighting and closed her eyes and mouth. She didn't want to die with mud clouding her eyes and coating her tongue.

But she didn't die. As she held onto her knees, her rounded back bobbed to the surface of the water. Instinctively she turned her face to the side and breathed. A white haze filled her vision. She tried to lift her head, but as soon as she moved her arms and legs, her leg muscles seized up and she began sinking again.

Ashley stopped flailing and tried to remember what she had learned from her very first swim class. Clenching her teeth against the pain in her legs and the burning in her lungs, she rounded over her legs again, into a dead man's float.

She bobbed to the surface.

She struggled against the urge to fight the water and to hurry. Using gentle, waving motions with her hands, she propelled herself to the opposite bank. She forced herself to wait for each breath, keeping her face down in the water when she wasn't breathing.

Maneuvering so that she lay along the gentle slope of the opposite bank, she lifted her face free, sucking at the air, desperate to breathe, to stop the pain, to recover enough strength to get to the house in time.

Ashley's body was an enormous weight she dragged up the slope of the bank. She couldn't straighten her legs. With trembling hands, she grabbed a root curving out of the bank and heaved herself out of the creek. The water seemed to tug at her, releasing her unwillingly, but then it fell away with a splash.

Half-crouching, she inched up the gentle slope to the top of the bank. She lay there, panting, as she looked down.

The water swirled in slow eddies. As she struggled for breath, the surface smoothed and the mud began to settle, erasing any sign that she had nearly died there.

Helpless tears filled her eyes as she rolled onto her

back and kneaded her thighs. Since her dream the night before last, she had assumed that there was an innate goodness or purity about the water that would somehow cancel out the demon's evil. But the water wasn't innately *good* or *bad:* it was just water.

Vernettie had been right. The dreams were full of portents and signs that Ashley didn't yet understand. Tears welled up and ran down her cheeks. Her dream of the demon and her interpretation of it were the only weapons she had to use against him. If her interpretation should prove wrong, then she had no other protection against him to offer Nikki.

Water trickled from Ashley's hair and clothes as she finally pushed herself to her feet. Trembling, still unable to straighten her legs completely, she took a step. She had to make it back to the house. Even if Rosamar had reached the dam by now, Ashley was still closer to the house than the others were.

Besides, if her dreams left her unsure of how to stop the demon, the others had even less to guide them.

She started forward, but stepped on a sticker. Hopping in place, trying to pull out the sticker, she realized that she might as easily have stepped on something more dangerous—a snake.

Limping back to where she had thrown her shoes, she sat down, then pulled on the first one, not pausing to wipe away the mud caked between her toes. Her fingers felt clumsy, thicker than normal. By the time that she had finished with the first one, her legs trembled, but the pain in her muscles had eased some.

She reached for the second shoe. Just then, some instinct made her pause. The hairs on her forearms and at the nape of her neck rose.

He must be near.

Water dripped from Ashley's bangs into her eyes. She shook her head, droplets spraying out from the ends of her hair. She studied the brush ahead of her, then turned her head slowly from side to side, looking at the foliage along the bank of the creek.

Nothing. She saw nothing.

She breathed in, expanding her lungs slowly, tasting the air. She smelled nothing unusual.

Still, she knew that he must be somewhere on the house side of the creek. The prickling of the skin at the back of her neck told her that she was right. Hurriedly, she pulled on the shoe, not bothering to tie the laces. She started forward again, staggering.

Nothing happened at first. After hobbling for a few minutes, her leg muscles loosened enough so that she could make faster progress. Four or five minutes later, she glimpsed a stand of trees to her left where the cabin had once stood. She cut in that direction, coming out on the path that she and the others had followed two days earlier, going in the opposite direction.

Then, up ahead, near a turn in the path, she thought that she saw a shadow disengage itself from the trees. She stopped, her heart bucking against her ribs. When she did, the shadow glided back toward the trees.

A wind caught the trees along either side of the path, swaying the upper branches. Shadows shifted, melding with one another and then breaking apart. Ashley squinted, staring into the undergrowth. Tendrils of fear brushed her skin, setting it quivering. She hesitated to move until she was sure of what she had seen, but finally there was nothing to do but go on. She spurted ahead, running past the spot where she had seen the shadow.

A moment later, she heard the first thin wail.

"Nikki," she whispered. From that moment on, she ran with no thought other than getting to Nikki. She dug her hand into her side to press against the new pain blooming there. Sand flew out from her feet, kicked up by her awkward, shuffling movements.

She broke into the open, praying that Lucas and the others had reached the house before her. Vernettie's old truck stood on the driveway not far from Rosamar's car, with Nikki's carseat inside, but the lawn and the walkway were empty.

Ashley slowed to a walk. Her lips and tongue went cold. From somewhere inside the house, Nikki cried with long pauses between each breath, as if she had been crying a long time.

Ashley looked up at the stucco-clad walls of her house. "Vernettie!" she screamed.

No one answered. Turning toward the woods, she yelled, "Lucas!" There was no answer from that direction either.

She stood on the driveway, clenching and unclenching her hands. "Someone tell me what's happening!" she shouted. She could face whatever had to be faced if only she knew what it was. But there was no one to tell her, and finally there was nothing left for her to do but to go inside. She started in.

When the telephone rang a few seconds later, Ashley had already made it up the stairs to the first landing. The sudden noise started her heart thumping wild in her chest. She stumbled, her breath hissing through her clenched teeth. Recovering her balance, she thought of going to answer the telephone, of begging whoever was on the other end for help.

But no one could help. After a last glance toward the kitchen, she hurried up the final flight of stairs. The telephone stopped ringing, and her father's voice repeated a recorded message. His distant, disembodied voice and Nikki's thin cries from somewhere upstairs contributed to the eerie, frightening atmosphere as Ashley left the stairway and started down the hall.

She crept down the hall toward the nursery, then passed it without looking inside. Nikki's cries seemed to be coming from farther away, from beyond the turn in the hall.

Downstairs the rumble of their father's voice, no longer distinguishable as distinct words, went on and on.

Ashley inched around the corner where the hall turned, and looked down the short portion which led to the master suite. When she found the hallway to be clear, she made her way into her parents' bedroom.

Nikki's cries were louder now and seemed to be echoing off the tiled walls of the bathroom. Ashley faced the closed bathroom door.

Then, reaching out with a trembling, sweat-slicked hand, she turned the knob. The catch released and the door swung open.

Vernettie stood in the middle of the sunken tub, holding Nikki tightly against her shoulder. Without the muffling door, Nikki's screams were piercing.

But she was alive. Ashley closed her eyes in relief, then opened them again.

She took a step forward, beginning to smile, then stopped.

The tub was filled. Water rose to the level of Vernettie's knees. The bottom of her skirt was wet and clung to her legs. Her long feet were bare, her shoes and socks laid carefully on the tile surround. She had backed into a corner of the tub, as far away from the outer sides as possible.

Sudden, wrenching guilt swallowed Ashley. She had told Vernettie that the demon was afraid of water. She was responsible for Vernettie's false confidence in a bathtub full of water. Holding back her sobs, Ashley walked to the side of the tub. She stooped, picking up a rolled towel from the basket beside the dressing table, then put the towel down on the tile surround.

"It wouldn't have worked," she said, shouting to make herself heard over Nikki's screams. She held out her arms, taking Nikki. "He could have reached across and grabbed her out of your arms."

Nikki's face was red, but she stilled and looked up at Ashley, as if she wanted to hear what was being said. She hiccupped with a convulsive hitching of her chest.

"It did work," Vernettie said. "I found out something about him today that we didn't know before. He has to take this one alive."

Ashley felt a premonitory chill move down her spine. "What are you saying?" she asked.

"He was out there all right. Even I could feel his presence, but he didn't try to get Nikki. And that's because he knew what I would do if he stepped foot in this house. I might not have your powers, but I still have my wits about me. If he had tried to come anywhere near this baby, I would have put her under the water."

Stunned, Ashley watched as Vernettie lifted her skirt and twisted the hem. She tried to imagine some meaning for Vernettie's words other than the terrible one she had understood: that Vernettie would have

111

drowned Nikki rather than let the demon have her. She couldn't think of one. Vernettie sounded tired but calm. She lifted each section of her skirt and squeezed the water, exposing thin legs, white thighs, and bony, misshapen knees. There was a hardness in her expression that Ashley had never seen there.

Maybe Vernettie was as crazy as Clay thought she was.

Ashley pressed her hand against Nikki's back, feeling the jerk of the baby's ribs as the hiccups caught her. Then a thought came to Ashley of its own volition. There *was* a way to prevent Nikki from suffering what Elizabeth had suffered, and Vernettie had named that way.

If flooding the creek failed to stop the demon, if he were coming for Nikki and they could not stop him, then they could still protect her from suffering as Elizabeth had.

Only, Ashley doubted that she had Vernettie's strength. She doubted if she could save Nikki from one death by threatening her with another.

THIRTEEN

Vernettie climbed out of the tub, bracing her hands on the tile surround. The surface of the water swirled in eddies, chilling Ashley with its reminder of what had happened to her in the creek. Both she and Nikki had been in danger of dying on this day, and both by drowning.

Then anger overwhelmed the fear. "Why did you bring her home?" she shouted at Vernettie. "If you had kept her at your house, like we decided, she would be safe, and we wouldn't have to be thinking about things like this." Ashley looked down at Nikki, who watched her with wide-open, startled eyes. Suddenly Ashley wished that she hadn't said those words so loudly.

Vernettie dried her feet and legs with slow deliberation, then looked up as she answered. "The cellular phone wasn't working. The batteries must have been dead. By the time I figured it out and checked the messages here, your parents had been calling for a couple of hours. The last message said that your father was winding up a meeting early this afternoon and would be home shortly. I had to hurry back or they'd find out what we were up to."

"I don't care," Ashley said. "You have to take

Nikki back to your house and keep her there overnight and tomorrow while we finish work on the dam. I'll think of something to tell my parents.''

Vernettie sat down on the edge of the tub. She reached for her shoes and socks, but then held them in her lap without slipping them on.

"He was out there, Vernettie. He was just waiting for a chance at her. I think that he's figured out that I can't do anything to him yet.''

"Or else he's figured out that you can,'' Vernettie said, looking up, her eyes narrowed and her forehead furrowed with worry lines. "He might be getting desperate and ready to risk it before you learn any more. Or maybe his days above ground are limited. There's just a whole lot of things that we don't know about him. Maybe he dies if he doesn't find a baby soon enough. You're not practiced enough at this yet to know what he's thinking. I keep telling you, don't go off half-cocked.''

Ashley looked down at her younger sister. "Take her to your house and keep her there, Vernettie,'' she said, her words clipped.

"Doesn't matter what you tell your parents, they're going to come get her.''

"Then don't take her to your house. Take her someplace where they won't find you.'' Ashley knew that she was talking too fast, almost spitting out the words.

The faster she talked, the calmer Vernettie's face seemed to grow. Seeing her stubborn composure, anger bubbled thick and scalding in Ashley's chest. Ashley wanted guidelines for what she should do. She wanted all of this to be over and done with and she wanted no responsibility in what happened. If that wasn't possible—and she knew that it wasn't—

114

then she wanted Vernettie to go along with the one thing that seemed plausible.

Then the anger was gone as quickly as it had risen. Without Vernettie, she might never have known that the dreams were revealing information that might save Nikki. Her little sister might already be dead.

Vernettie had been watching her. She spoke now. "It's not that I haven't already considered running away with Nicole. I have. I calculate that I've got enough money saved to go across country somewhere and keep her and me away at least three or four years, or until you let us know it's safe to come back. But your parents have more money. No matter where I hid out, they would find us. And then I'd be locked up for kidnapping, and you'd have no one to help you protect Nicole."

As if hearing her name had roused her into fretfulness again, Nikki fussed, digging her toes into Ashley's chest and climbing her shoulder like a frightened kitten.

Vernettie looked down at the shoes and socks that she still held in her lap. She glanced up at Nikki, then met Ashley's gaze.

"She knows something bad is happening, doesn't she?" Ashley asked.

"Yes, I suspect she does," Vernettie said. "Not in words, mind, but she's feeling the danger." She breathed in and then out and her shoulders slumped. She brushed her shoes and socks off her lap and onto the floor. "Let's go," she said, standing. "We'll give it a try."

Downstairs, waiting for Vernettie to make her slow descent, Ashley toured the rooms, looking out of the windows. Nikki's cries grew louder and more insistent. Ashley wondered if she were hungry, and went

115

to the kitchen to get a bottle. She took the bottle from the refrigerator and Vernettie's keys from the peg where she kept them during the day, then crept near the stained glass window. She peered out at the trees, the slash of green lawn, the brown of the deck turned blue in its frame of purple glass. The answering machine beeped, as if it were measuring how little time they had left in which to get Nikki to safety.

If the demon were anywhere near the house, then he was hidden where Ashley couldn't see him.

When she emerged from the kitchen hallway and into the open foyer, Vernettie was halfway to the front door, still barefoot. "Come on," Vernettie said.

Ashley let Vernettie go first. When nothing happened, Ashley broke into an awkward running gait. She thought of the demon waiting underground through all those years, with only a skin of dried mud separating him from the world and his next victim, and the thought prompted her to press forward despite her exhaustion. She passed Vernettie.

Rosamar's car was parked near the house, but Vernettie's old Chevy truck was parked farther away, canted to the left because of the slope of the drive. The asphalt had softened in the afternoon's heat. Ashley could see it dented beneath the tires of the vehicles. It gave beneath her when she stepped down.

Nikki stopped crying again and lay still against Ashley's chest, her head thumping softly against Ashley's collarbone with each jogging step. It was as if the heat outside stupified her.

Then, just as Ashley passed the planting of St. Joseph's Coat, just when she was beginning to think that she might make it to the truck without incident, she heard Vernettie grunt.

Time slowed.

Ashley stopped, settled Nikki securely on her shoulder, then turned.

Vernettie stood in nearly the same position as she had on that morning when Ashley had come outside at dawn and found her staring into the stand of trees on the west side of the property. Her thin lips were firmed. The tired slump of her shoulders was replaced by a rigid posture. She seemed to have added height and mass and strength all at once.

Ashley turned so that she had a clear view into the woods, where Vernettie was staring. Her heart dropped through her chest.

He was there, a black shadow beneath the largest oak. His gaze seemed to be fixed on Nikki. Ashley could feel his ugly wanting through the distance that separated them.

"Vernettie," she said, still watching him. She dropped the plastic bottle to the ground, heard it bounce, and then held her hand out to the side, jiggling the keys. She tossed them back in Vernettie's direction, but heard them hit the asphalt. "Get the keys and get the truck started," she said.

Vernettie moved past Ashley, shambling with a quick gait toward the truck. Ashley concentrated, trying to quiet the tendrils of fear that pierced her brain and her heart. She searched through her memories of her dreams for something that might help, and latched onto the image of herself laughing at the demon. If he could perceive her thoughts, then she wanted that image to be the one that he read there.

Nikki pulled her legs in, digging her toes into Ashley's ribs as the demon moved, circling back through the woods. Ashley's heart squeezed with fear when she lost sight of him in the shadows.

Vernettie reached the truck and paused to look back.

A blackbird flew away, angling over the driveway in front of Ashley and then rising on the air currents. When he was far overhead, he let out a piercing caw, circled once, and then was gone.

When Ashley looked down again, the demon had moved out of the concealing foliage and shadows and stood on the edge of the woods, between her and the truck.

If she tried to reach the truck, she feared that he would intercept her.

His foul odor billowed out toward Ashley. Nikki sneezed as the stench engulfed them, and then she fussed, scrubbing her nose back and forth across Ashley's shoulder.

Ashley stared, unable to move. She had seen the demon three times now, but she had never allowed herself to look at him too closely. She had thought at first that he had been burned and then later that he wasn't human, but she saw now that she had been wrong both times. He was human, or had been, and his flesh wasn't burned, but rotting.

Ashley heard the truck door open and shut, but she didn't dare look away. He had been human, but now he was something different. He was a demon, the evil one whose coming Grandmother Birdie had foretold.

He started forward, bone rubbing against bone.

Ashley's stomach went cold with fear and revulsion. He wasn't alive. Not the way that she was, and Nikki was. She believed that she knew now what he needed from Nikki: her life force, to counter the mortification of his flesh; her purity, to counter his corruption.

Ashley looked to either side of her as he moved out from the trees in which he had hidden. She had no weapon, no special knowledge to use against him. Out here, there was not even the last resort of a bathtub full of water. She turned back to the house, trying to remember if Vernettie had emptied the tub.

It was then that she heard Rosamar shout.

Footsteps pounded down the drive, coming toward her and then passing her. Out of the corner of her eye, she saw blurs that resolved into Lucas, Rosamar, and Clay. They came to a stop farther down the drive, between her and the demon. Lucas and Rosamar clasped each other's shoulders, standing together, but Clay waved his hands in front of him, as if the creature he was trying to frighten away were a stray dog that had wandered out of the woods. Poor Clay, Ashley thought. He always searched for a logical explanation, and he wasn't going to find one this time.

Before Ashley could retreat farther toward the house, Vernettie's truck roared to life. Ashley glanced at it long enough to see Vernettie's grim expression through the windshield, her knotted hands on the steering wheel.

Shouting instructions to each other, Lucas, Rosamar, and Clay arranged themselves into a gauntlet along the edge of the drive.

Ashley wished fiercely, with a longing that tightened her stomach, that Vernettie would run her heavy, old truck over the flower beds and onto the portion of the lawn where the demon waited, yet she sensed that it would do no good to try to run him down. Stopping him couldn't be that simple. Somehow he must have learned the secret power of preserving and regenerating his body beyond his natural death.

He moved again. Ashley backed up, feeling as if he and she were participating in a choreographed dance of death.

"Just stay where you are," Lucas called. "We'll help you get Nicole into the truck."

Vernettie drove straight toward Ashley, angling across the drive.

"Circle around so that you're headed out toward the road," Ashley yelled to her. She felt the passage of the old truck, the wave of heat emanating from the expanse of metal. Lucas and Rosamar ran past her while Clay stayed where he was. She heard Lucas and Rosamar moving behind her, but she did not look away from the demon.

The breath wheezed in and out of his chest. His nostrils were clogged with dirt, and the air reached his lungs by way of holes gouged in his neck. His musk enveloped Ashley and Nikki. The baby coughed and then seemed to hold her breath.

After that, everything happened so quickly that Ashley could only react without reasoning out her decision.

She pushed back, desperate to get far enough away so that she and Nikki could breathe clean air. Moving too fast, she thudded into Lucas, who must have run up behind her. He caught her and kept her and Nikki from falling.

But the demon rushed toward them.

Perhaps it was Vernettie's example that prompted Ashley to do what she did then.

Pushing away from Lucas, she grabbed Nikki's ankle in one hand and swung the baby upside down, suspended above the asphalt. "I'll kill her," she shouted. "I'll drop her onto the driveway."

Nikki sucked in a surprised breath, but that single breath was followed by a long, shocked silence. Ashley's heart flopped loosely. She didn't dare look at Nikki, didn't dare let herself feel concern.

She sensed rather than saw Lucas shift behind her. "Don't try to take her," she said to him. "You don't understand. I can't let her die like Elizabeth did."

The demon was so close that his cold exhalations smothered Ashley, but she had stopped his forward advance. The withered look of his flesh sickened Ashley. Her arm trembled from Nikki's weight. The muscles in her shoulders, already strained from the work at the dam, spasmed painfully.

Lucas touched the small of Ashley's back, then slid his hand along the length of her arm, grasping her wrist and supporting some of Nikki's weight. "I'll lead you to the truck," he whispered.

Ashley followed Lucas's guidance, never letting her gaze veer from the demon's, keeping her own body between his and Nikki's. Nikki threw her arms out to the side, but other than that she didn't struggle. It seemed to Ashley that she barely breathed.

Ashley's gaze was drawn to the demon's hands. The thickened nails were rimmed with dirt. Ashley thought of him clawing away the dirt as he rose to the surface of his lair, and felt her stomach heave.

She must have made a sound, because Lucas moved his hand up, enveloping her hand in his own, squeezing her fingers between his hand and Nikki's ankle. She swallowed the bitter taste that had risen to the back of her throat. "Don't stop me from letting go of her if I need to," she pleaded.

"You won't need to," he said. "We're nearly

there. Rosamar's in the truck with Vernettie, waiting. She's got the door open."

Ashley nodded, hearing now the thrumming of the truck's motor. Sunlight fell across the demon, revealing the shape of browbone and of jawline beneath the ravaged face. Mesmerized, caught by something in the shapes that she saw there, Ashley stared.

He reached for Nikki. His fingers with their fearful, raking nails curved toward her.

Lucas reacted, loosening his fingers from around hers.

Ashley gasped. The time had come to make a decision. She couldn't let the demon have Nikki.

Then there was no decision to make. Ashley's numbed fingers refused to function. Nikki slipped from her grasp.

Someone screamed, but Ashley was never sure whether it was herself or Rosamar.

Lucas caught Nikki when she was halfway through her plunging fall. He cradled her to his chest, the expression in his brown eyes flat and stricken when Ashley turned to look at him.

But power and exultation surged through Ashley. They had stopped the demon in the act of grabbing Nikki. "We can do it!" she screamed, facing the demon. "We can keep her from you!"

She heard a door slam, and then the revving of a motor. The truck pulled away, the tires squealing as they caught traction. The truck sped past the dip in the drive, making the turn onto the road.

The demon turned. His clacking, disjointed stride carried him toward the woods, within two or three feet of where Clay stood, open-mouthed. As he entered the shadows below the trees, he paused and looked back at Ashley.

With a shaking arm, she pointed to the spot where the driveway dipped down, following the gentle curve of the creek bed. "Tomorrow that's going to be flooded," she said. "You won't be able to get to her, ever again."

He watched her a moment longer. Then he was gone into the shadows.

FOURTEEN

Relief turned Ashley's legs rubbery. She went into Lucas's arms, breathing in his scent of sweat and stone dust. She was trembling, and she could feel him trembling, too. "I want to go inside," she whispered to him. "I don't want to be out here where he is any longer."

As they entered through the still-open door, the telephone rang again. Ashley limped into the kitchen, Lucas and Clay following, just as her father's recorded message ended with a beep. Her mother's voice spoke into the room. Ashley listened but didn't pick up the receiver.

"Vernettie, we've been trying to contact you most of the afternoon," her mother said. Ashley could hear the strain and irritation in her voice. "If you've been out, please call Mr. Morgan on the car phone and then call me. He's on his way to the house now."

Ashley looked out of the stained glass window without seeing anything. In her mind, she kept replaying that terrible scene outside, with those hands with the terrible, raking nails reaching for Nikki. Lucas and Clay were silent, too, perhaps reliving their own particular moments of horror, but Lucas stood just behind her, his hand on her arm just above her elbow. She could hear his ragged breathing.

She longed to lean against him and go on leaning against him, but she had decisions to make. There was still something that had to be done, and soon. Turning to him, she said, "If we don't come up with a good reason for Vernettie to keep Nikki away from here, my parents are going to bring her back."

She looked from Lucas to Clay. Lucas's blanched complexion and Clay's white lips indicated their shock at what they had seen outside. "We can't let them bring her back, yet," she said, hoping that her words were registering with them. "He'll be waiting for her."

Lucas nodded. "I wanted to help you, but I never really believed . . ." he said, but then he stopped and wiped a hand across his mouth. "Tell us what to do," he said. His voice was flat, with no intonations in his words.

"I don't know what to do, Lucas. You have to help me think of something," Ashley said. "You and Clay both." She moved around the kitchen, touching the granite cabinet tops here and there with her fingertips, hoping that something would communicate itself to her through touch, if not by sight.

Clay touched her shoulder. He had taken off his cap and held it in his hand. His hair was flattened into a bowl shape and darkened by sweat. "I've got an idea," he said.

The answering machine beeped. Ashley turned her head and waves of pain moved across her sore muscles. She looked from Clay to the machine and then back to him. "Tell me," she said.

Clay nodded. "The other day, your dad was saying that he didn't have chicken pox when he was a kid.

We could tell him that my grandmother thinks that Nicole broke out with it today."

Ashley was already shaking her head. "My mother would be at Vernettie's house in ten minutes flat if we told her that Nikki was sick. You know how she feels about Vernettie's homemade remedies. And she thinks Vernettie's too old to be taking care of a baby by herself. That's why she's hiring a nanny."

Lucas opened the cabinet under the sink and squatted in front of it. "Got any insecticide?" he asked over his shoulder. "We could spray it all around the house and tell your father that the fumes were too strong for Nicole."

"No, my parents don't use commercial insecticides," Ashley answered. "They mix up something on their own whenever we have problems with ants or anything." She could hear the flat sound of her voice. The answering machine beeped again and she looked down at the red triangle of light cast on her leg by the stained glass window. She felt panicky, but also removed from the panic, as if it were happening to someone else. It was almost too late to do anything. Two or three minutes had gone by and they were still standing in the kitchen. She twisted her leg, watching the flicker of red light across her skin. It reminded her of a flame.

Then, as she thought of flames, and linked that thought to Lucas's idea of fumes, she knew that she had hit upon a plan that might work. She looked from the red triangle on her leg to the oven. When Lucas shut the cabinet door and stood up, she grabbed his arm. "We could burn something in the oven," she said. "If there was enough smoke. . . ."

"Damn," Clay said, interrupting. He grinned. "You're on to an idea that might work. It has to be more than something burning in the oven, though. We have to set something on fire.''

"Wait," Lucas said. "Let's think about this a minute. Maybe there's something less drastic we can do. This isn't like flooding the driveway for a few days."

Clay shook his head. "You saw that thing out there. We have to do something drastic. Besides, I'm not talking about setting the whole house on fire. Just part of it."

Lucas shook his head, his lips bunched and his eyebrows drawn together. "It's too risky. A fire's too hard to control. Let's just stop and think a minute. There has to be something else."

"There isn't time for anything else," Clay shouted, waving his long arms toward Ashley. "Didn't you hear what Ashley said? We have to hurry!"

"Yes, I heard," Lucas said, and his voice was gruff, almost a growl. "I've heard her from the time she started telling us what she had seen up there in that nursery. I didn't always believe all of it, but I heard her and I was willing to help. Which is more than you can say. But this is too important to mess up. Quit trying to play the hero and help us think."

Clay's face reddened. He lowered his arms and tilted his head back. Instead of exploding, as Ashley expected, he blew out a big breath of air and said, "You're right."

"Stop arguing. Please," Ashley said. Her voice was quiet, but both Lucas and Clay looked at her and then down at the floor.

After a moment's silence, Clay spoke and his voice was calm. "We could smoke up the house. Burn some paper, maybe. In a trash can. Or a wastebasket, even. The central air conditioning system would carry the smoke through the house."

Lucas sighed. "Not even trash in a trash can, unless we have the fire extinguisher with us," he said.

"Good enough," Clay answered.

"There's an extinguisher just inside the pantry door," Ashley said.

"Stay here. I'll get it," Lucas said.

The answering machine beeped. Ashley glanced at it, then opened a drawer, pushing things aside in her hurry to find the box of matches that Vernettie kept there.

Clay reached for them, but then Ashley remembered something and pulled the matchbox away from him in reflex.

"I forgot. We have zoned air conditioning," she said. Her throat felt swollen with disappointment, her tongue thick and slow. "Three separate zones. One for the whole downstairs, but two separate ones upstairs. They work independently of each other."

"The smoke won't carry through the whole house," Lucas said, coming back. Then, almost as soon as he had finished speaking, his eyebrows went up. "Are your bedroom and the nursery on the same zone?" he asked.

"Most of the rooms upstairs are on that zone," she said. "Everything but the master suite." Clay didn't wait for her to finish. He took the matches from her and started off in a jog down the hallway that led to the foyer.

"Let's go," Lucas said, starting after him with the fire extinguisher held under his arm. "He still might burn the house down."

Ashley reached her room only seconds after Clay and Lucas, but Clay had already opened the box of matches, and Lucas had pulled her wastebasket out from underneath her desk. "My grandmother's too efficient," Clay said. "It's empty. Quick. What can we use to start a fire?"

Ashley glanced at her desk and saw something immediately. She grabbed the workbook and loose worksheets from her correspondence course. Clay took the workbook from her, ripping off the slick cover and dropping it onto her desk. While he tore the pages apart and dropped them into the wastebasket, Ashley crumpled the loose worksheets. Lucas set the extinguisher on top of her desk and took one of the matches from the open box. As soon as Ashley dropped in the last page, he struck the match.

Clay moved quickly, catching his wrist. "Not yet," he said.

The match flamed close to Lucas's fingertips. He pulled his wrist out of Clay's grasp, shook the match until the flame went out, then set it on the edge of her desk with the burned end hanging over the edge. "Why not?" he asked.

"I changed my mind," Clay said, picking up the wastebasket. "Papers won't make enough smoke."

He tried to take the matches, too, but Lucas snatched them up and held them. "I told you that's all I was going to agree to," Lucas said.

"We're wasting time," Ashley said.

Then, thinking she heard something, she ran out into the hall, listened for a moment, then came back. Lucas and Clay were over near her window, arguing, but both looked up at her. "No, my father's not here yet," she said.

Clay lifted the ends of the gauzy fabric that hung on either side of her window. As he did, Ashley looked around her room, at all of the things that she had collected. She thought about the valuable photographs that lined the hall, the lithographs downstairs, and she knew that none of it mattered when Nikki's life was weighed in the balance. "Maybe we ought to burn it down for real," she said. "It would take my parents months, a year, to rebuild. We would have to live somewhere else."

Lucas looked at her, then shook his head. "It might never get rebuilt. There are ways to find out if someone sets a fire, you know. Your parents wouldn't get the insurance money. Look, I'll tell your father what I saw. Clay and I both will."

"He won't believe you, Lucas."

"I'll make him believe me."

Clay still held the end of the drapes. He made a motion for the matches, but Lucas held them away.

"He didn't believe *me,*" Ashley said. "It's not easy to believe this. You had a hard time with it, too, remember?"

Lucas hesitated. She could see that he wanted to say something, but there wasn't anything to say. She was telling the truth. After a moment, he opened the box. "Okay," he said as he struck the match. "I'll go along with it. Not the whole house, though," he said. "We're just creating smoke, that's all." He held the match to a corner of one of the pieces of crumpled paper. When the flame caught, he dropped the match into the wastebasket, and Clay draped the ends of the fabric across the top of the papers. Ashley heard the small pop when the rest of the papers caught fire.

"I'll get the extinguisher," Clay said, glancing at Lucas. "We're going to need it in a minute."

A scorch mark bloomed on the drapery fabric where it was draped across the mouth of the wastebasket, then widened slowly, as if it were a flower whose petals were opening. Lucas took Ashley's hand and squeezed. "I love you, Ashley Morgan," he whispered, so low that she wasn't sure at first that she had heard correctly. "And I tried to believe you. Does that count for anything?"

"Yes, it does," Ashley said, squeezing back. "It counts for a lot." Then, before she or Lucas could say more, Clay came back with the extinguisher. The drapery caught with a whoosh. Flames climbed the fabric toward the top of the window, charring the sheetrock as it rose.

"Back up," Lucas said, tugging Ashley's hand.

Patches of charred paper floated upward from the wastebasket. A piece of burning fabric fell to the floor, melting a small hole in the carpet. Tendrils of black, sooty smoke curled at ceiling level. Then, just when Clay started to release the catch on the extinguisher, the fire suddenly began to lessen in intensity.

Ashley looked toward the dressing room that connected her room to the nursery. "There's not enough smoke," she said. "There has to be more." She turned in a circle, surveying her room. "Will the bedcover burn?" she asked, running to the bed.

Clay ran ahead. "Try this," he said, tossing a pillow to her. "The filling should smoke."

It did. Although she and Lucas couldn't seem to set the pillow aflame, it smoldered with an acrid smoke that set Ashley and the others coughing. Holding it away from her body with one hand, and burying her nose in the crook of the other elbow, Ashley walked through the dressing room, the bathroom, and then out into the connecting nursery, waving the pillow back and forth. Lucas and Clay followed, Clay still holding the extinguisher. "It's working," Clay said, his words muffled by the hand he held over his mouth and nose.

Then, unexpectedly, flames began to break out from the pillow covering.

Ashley screamed and almost dropped it, but suddenly Lucas grabbed it from her, then ran into the hall. Ashley and Clay ran after him.

"The fire alarm," he shouted over his shoulder. "It should have gone off if there was a lot of smoke."

Then, as Lucas lifted the pillow above his head, Ashley heard the sound that she had been dreading all along. It was her father's car horn sounding in a long bleat as the car approached the house.

Before Ashley or the others could move, flames shot from both the top and the sides of the pillow. Yelling a warning, Ashley tried to bat it out of Lucas's hands. Clay fumbled with the extinguisher. The alarm came on, adding to the confusion of sound. Lucas twisted away, running back into Ashley's bedroom. She tried to follow him, but Clay pushed ahead of her, turning and signaling her to stay back.

His behavior confused her at first. Out of a sense of surprise, she did as he indicated, but then she realized what might have prompted him to try to keep her out.

Lucas's hands must be burned. Clay hadn't wanted her to see.

Ignoring his instructions, she raced into the room after him. Clay had put down the extinguisher and was stomping out the flames on the pillow. Lucas stood a few feet away, holding his hands out in front of him, palms down, fingers spread.

Ashley's mouth went dry. "Oh, Lucas," she said.

His hands were beet-red, obviously burned. She couldn't see any blisters, but perhaps they hadn't had time to form. "Why did you hold on to the pillow so long?" she asked.

The front door was flung open downstairs. "Ashley? Vernettie?" her father called.

"I couldn't drop it out in the hall," Lucas said, speaking in a strained whisper. "Your father would know that we had set the fire intentionally if he saw the pillow out there."

"Ashley?" her father called again.

Clay looked up from examining the pillow. "Go," he said, his voice harsh. "Keep him downstairs as long as you can while we set some things up."

Ashley nodded. "I'm coming," she yelled. She turned toward the door, but then stopped and told Lucas, "Dad will help me to take you to the hospital. We'll get your hands taken care of."

Lucas shook his head. His mouth was squared in a grimace that showed his teeth. "Don't tell him about my hands. Don't tell anyone. Vernettie was supposed to have been here when the fire started, remember? She would have done something about my hands."

Ashley's breath hissed between her teeth as she hurried from the room. If they had come up with another plan, as Lucas had wanted, then he wouldn't be injured now.

The hall was hazy with smoke. Ashley ran through it, and then met her father at the first landing on the stairs. "What's happened?" he shouted over the sound of the alarm. He tried to squeeze past her, but she blocked him.

"There was a fire in my room," she said, her mouth close to his ear. From where they were standing, the sound of the alarm was deafening. "Clay and Lucas helped me to put it out."

Her father slipped past her, then stopped and turned his face up, looking toward the top of the stairs. His whole body went still. "Where's Nicole?" he asked.

"She's not here!" Ashley shouted. "Vernettie took her away. Because of the smoke."

"Why didn't Vernettie call us?" her father asked. He didn't wait for an answer, but ran up the stairs and reached for the smoke alarm on the wall at the top of the stairs. Ashley remained behind, watching him, suddenly wary. *Why didn't Vernettie call?* What reason could she give?

The alarm went off, leaving behind a ringing silence. "It's my fault that you didn't get a call," she said, moving up the stairs. The smoke and her anxiety to say the right thing tightened her throat muscles, so that her words came out in a croak. "Vernettie sent me to do it, but I forgot. Everything was so confused."

Sooner or later, her father would remember all the calls that he and Ashley's mother had placed to the house, which no one had answered. There were too many inconsistencies in her story, Ashley thought, too many points she hadn't had time to work out. If her father were to double-check her story with Vernettie right now, then he would learn that Vernettie knew nothing at all about a fire.

Suddenly she remembered something else. Vernettie's shoes and socks were still on the floor in the master bathroom. If she didn't manage to hide them, how was she going to explain that?

Ashley's father turned and walked the short distance to her bedroom. He walked in and she followed.

Lucas and Clay stood near the window. Both held

hand towels from the bathroom over their mouths and noses, as if they had needed protection from the smoke, but they lowered them as soon as Ashley's father had had time to notice. Ashley saw that Lucas was careful to keep the towel draped so that it hid his hands.

"Boys," her father said, nodding to Lucas and Clay. His manner was grim as he walked to the window and stood between them. He looked down at the wastebasket, then up at the wall and the tatters of drapery that still hung from the scorched wooden rod.

"It must have been an electrical fire," Clay said, pointing to a lamp cord. Ashley saw a break in the cord. Even to her, it looked as if it had been hastily frayed and then rubbed with soot. "We managed to get it unplugged and the fire put out. We smothered it with that pillow over there."

Ashley's stomach twisted as she watched her father study the circle of soot that had formed on the ceiling. Something was wrong. She could tell that he didn't believe the story that he was hearing. He picked up the frayed section of the lamp cord, glanced at the wastebasket, and then turned to look at her desk.

Lucas shot Ashley a stricken glance that told her that he realized that something was wrong, too. Clay hunched his shoulders, then turned to look out the window.

There hadn't been time to do any more than had been done, but Ashley saw now how useless their efforts had been. The wastebasket, the drapery, the matches: all pointed to the fact that this was no accidental fire. Her stomach churned, as if she had swallowed something cold and oily and vile.

Turning away from the window, her father asked, "This isn't where you usually keep the wastebasket, is it?"

"No," Ashley whispered. When she saw the downward slope of his shoulders, the way his arms hung loosely at his sides, an undeserved shame slowed her heartbeat. She had been trying to save Nikki, but her father didn't know that and wouldn't believe her if she told him.

Her father turned, walking to the desk. He put his hand on the ripped workbook cover and stood looking down at it for a moment. Bending forward, he picked up the spent match that Lucas had placed on the desk. He held it in the palm of his hand, looking down at it. Ashley watched him and then, when she couldn't watch any longer, she looked at Lucas. He beckoned to her and she went to him.

Standing beside him, their arms touching, she felt the slow expansion of his chest as he breathed. She would need his strength. She had the dreams, but Lucas had the steadiness and loyalty that she needed to face what was happening.

"Did you set the fire?" her father asked, directing the question to her.

She decided not to deny it. "Yes," she said.

He had seen the torn workbook cover. She had told him only that morning how she felt about the course. Let him draw his own conclusion—even a false one—if it kept him from asking more questions about what had happened and why.

"Alone?" he asked, looking from her to Lucas and then to Clay. "Did you set it alone?"

"Yes."

"Tell him," Lucas said, his voice low.

Her father heard. "Tell me what?"

Ashley jammed her hands into the pockets of her shorts, but she didn't answer. She pressed closer to Lucas, hoping that her touch would somehow convey to him that he mustn't say anything either. They had very little to gain even if her father decided to help them fight the demon: they had everything to lose if he decided to bring Nikki back to the house or to stop the work on the dam. The risks were too great.

When she didn't answer, her father asked Clay, "Do you and Lucas have a way to get home?"

"I have a set of keys to Rosamar's car," Lucas answered. "She rode with Vernettie." He reached for his pocket, then made a sound under his breath. Ashley glanced up at him. His lips were white and set with pain.

Ashley's father took off his coat and held it loosely in his hands. "I think that it would be best if you boys left now," he said. "I'll see you tomorrow morning."

"I'll call you tonight," Lucas said to Ashley.

"I would prefer that you didn't," her father answered. "We have some talking to do. You can see her tomorrow."

When Lucas and Clay left the room, Ashley turned back to the window, staring out across the tops of the trees, down to where the creek bed wound through a lazy curve. Suddenly the shame abated and some of the heat went out of her face. Her parents might never know what had really happened today, but she could deal with their reaction.

She had dealt with worse in these last couple of weeks. She suspected that she would deal with worse yet in the coming days.

FIFTEEN

Ashley's parents did not insist that Nikki be brought back to the house that night. The smoky odor lingered through the evening, but they were less concerned with the smoke's effect on Nikki than with having uninterrupted time with Ashley. The night's discussion had ended only when she had agreed to attend counseling sessions if Dr. Varula thought them necessary.

When she could finally escape, she dragged herself upstairs. After a steaming bath that did little to ease the soreness in her muscles, she propped herself up in bed so that her shoulders were supported. There was nothing to be seen in her window except a reflection of the interior of her room: no stars, no moon, no tops of trees. The clouds that had rolled in that day had obscured it all, but still she stared out the window, trying to penetrate the darkness.

Then, slowly, the blackness outside seemed to lighten and change form and color and texture. The curling edges of green leaves emerged from the darkness and drew Ashley through the night sky to the dam.

She understood that she was dreaming. She let the dream come.

She stood alone on the bank as greenish-black

clouds swam through the air above her. It appeared to be neither night nor day, but some in-between hellish time that belonged only to dreams.

When she lowered her gaze, she saw that Grandmother Birdie stood on the opposite bank, her grey hair loosened by the wind and blowing back from her face, her head turned in Ashley's direction. Shadows painted the sockets of her eyes and the hollow of her mouth, so that her face resembled that of a skull.

Ashley became aware of the feathery touch of fingers against her forearm. She looked down and saw that she held Nikki in her arms. Nikki was awake and watching her. When Ashley looked up again, Grandmother Birdie nodded. Ashley felt as if the three of them were involved in some ceremony that she didn't understand, but that Vernettie's grandmother did.

Grandmother Birdie pointed down at the dry bed of the creek and spoke, intoning fierce words that resembled a curse. "Death and hell were cast into the lake of fire," she said. "This is the second death." Thunder rumbled in a growling accompaniment to her words.

Ashley backed away from the edge of the bank, frightened by Grandmother Birdie's long arm, by her bony, pointing finger, and by her words. The wind increased, whipping Ashley's hair into her eyes and blinding her.

An overwhelming, massive terror numbed her, and then she saw something that started her shaking. The dam was as they had left it that day, with the V-shaped channel pointing downward. Behind the dam, the water rose more quickly than seemed possible, pouring through the opening. The stones on either side bulged outward, then tumbled to the bottom of the bed on the creek side. Water surged through the opening, breaking out more stones.

Suddenly Nikki's weight left Ashley's arms. Ashley felt as if a vital part of her own body had been ripped out of her. A terrible grief tore at her, and she wailed a protest. The wind shrieked and a sudden rain lashed at her, mingling with her tears.

Grandmother Birdie tilted her head, the strange light catching her features, the luminescent shine of her wet skin replacing the shadows that had been there. Her face no longer looked like that of a skull, but still she looked drawn and tired and old. Her shoulders slumped. "Look," she called, and her voice was thin and quivery, as it had been in the other dream. Her arm trembled as she pointed.

Ashley obeyed, but when she had looked, her knees buckled. She slid to the ground and lay there.

Nikki was in the water.

Alone, and in the water. She seemed to be floating, held up by her spreading garments. Water swirled wildly around her. It could only be moments until she was pulled under.

Ashley tried to rise, but her legs cramped and her arms refused to support her weight. She rolled over and put her hands to her chest, her lungs burning as if she were the one fighting the water and not Nikki. Above her, black clouds swept across the sky, swirling and foaming. The roar of thunder filled the world, numbing her eardrums.

And then came Grandmother Birdie's voice, as if she had whispered her words into Ashley's ear. "Look," she said. "She has drawn him to her."

"No," Ashley screamed. She sensed Grandmother Birdie staring at her, commanding her to see. Twisting away, she grabbed a thin shrub, and somehow she summoned the strength to tear it from the sandy soil. She reached for more, covering herself with the

long, tapering leaves and reddish stems, trying to hide from Grandmother Birdie's gaze, from what Grandmother Birdie wanted her to see.

The shrubs changed form, the leaves crumbling and the stems lengthening, transforming themselves into vines that snaked around Ashley's body and throat. The shrubs that she had pulled over herself for protection now bound her to the ground. Horrified, Ashley then felt the sliding of smooth scales against her throat, the abhorrent chill of reptile flesh against her skin.

The vines had become snakes that coiled around her.

She opened her mouth to scream, but the snakes looped themselves around her neck, cutting off the passage of air into her lungs.

She bolted upright.

And was awake, in her own room, in the grey light of early day, with her pillow twisted in her hands and the taste of the cotton pillowcase and her own salty tears mingling in her mouth.

As the grey light outside her window gave way to an overcast dawn, Ashley lay in her bed, staring out the window. She couldn't shake the feelings of horror and helplessness that lingered after the dream. She turned over on her side, looked into the empty bassinet and shuddered.

Lying back, she touched her neck. She should have obeyed the old woman's command and looked into the water. Now she would never know what she had been meant to see.

Her legs ached when she moved them. She lay with a hand on her throat, closing her eyes, and let the weakness wash her back into sleep again.

Charnas opened his eyes when they lowered him onto the flat stone at the place of magic. The youth lowered him too quickly, letting the back of his head bang against the stone. The twigs and pebbles embedded in his torn back made him gasp with pain, but he was too weak to struggle. He shuddered in the cold grip of quickly approaching death. Although he knew it to be the day of the longest sun, the sun's warmth could not penetrate this chill of death.

Ashley groaned as she tossed on the bed. She wrapped her arms around her upper body, trying to warm herself.

Standing on the bank, the one-armed man began chanting as the sun descended toward the top of the forked pine on the opposite bank. Clouds massed in the sky behind him. Soon the rains would come and waters would flood the place of magic.

The youth leaned close to Charnas, pretending to position his arm more comfortably, but in reality whispering, "Die now, Charnas. Die before the ceremony is finished."

Charnas didn't want to die. He struggled to draw each rattling breath. The fever burned the moisture from his eyes. He blinked, trying to focus on the one-armed man. He heard the magic words that he chanted, but he did not know their meaning. He only knew that they were the words that would save him and his lineage from extinction.

Then the youth and the woman screamed and turned to flee. Not understanding, Charnas blinked, trying to moisten his eyes so that he might see more clearly. The youth and the woman fell onto the dry bed of the place of the magic waters. Writhing shapes covered their bodies. At first Charnas thought the waters had been released, but there were no water

142

sounds—only the sounds of their screams. Soon the screams stopped and Charnas heard only the chants of the one-armed man.

Ashley heard herself gasping in her sleep. She turned her head and tried to open her eyes, but then fell back into an exhausted stupor.

Charnas did not know how long the chanting had continued when he felt the first cool touch of a viper on his fevered skin. He twisted and moaned as one of them crawled upward across his chest. Others weighed down his limbs.

"Do not fight them," the companion of the one-armed man cautioned. It was the first time she had spoken. "Their poison will burn away the poison within you. Afterward, the magic waters will come, quenching the fire. Then you will have new life and new powers. The vipers will be your companions."

The chanting of the one-armed man continued as the body of the viper on his chest coiled, its head and tail upraised. Its rattles vibrated. The sound set up a painful thrumming in Charnas's chest. "No," he tried to whisper, but it was too late.

As the sun descended between the forks of the pine, the coiled viper struck Charnas in the throat. He exhaled, then found that he could not draw breath again. Panicked, he thrashed, grabbing at his throat. The sun's rays shone full on him, adding to the heat of his fever, to the heat that this new poison engendered in him. White heat burned in his chest, searing his lungs and driving the moisture from his tissues. He felt the steam rise from him. As he watched, he saw his skin and muscles wither as his life fluids escaped.

With a hoarse cry, Ashley sat up in bed, flinging off the covers.

SIXTEEN

When Lucas, Clay, and Rosamar arrived later that morning to continue work on the dam, Ashley was waiting by the front door, afraid to go outside alone. The overcast sky of the day before had been replaced by low black clouds piled in massive formations that reminded her of the storm clouds from both dreams. As she opened the front door and walked outside, she glanced up at the sky and then looked down at the ground.

Lucas and the others got out of the car and stood near it, watching her. She felt again the sense of ceremony and of strangeness that had permeated both dreams. Lucas was the first to approach her, coming over and then kissing her lightly. Her lips trembled under his.

Clay turned, facing into the woods. Rosamar walked over to stand near him.

"Lucas," Ashley whispered. "I made a terrible mistake last night. I had a dream about Vernettie's grandmother again. There was something that she wanted me to see, but I wouldn't look. Now I don't know what it was."

"Shhh!" Lucas said. He opened his arms to her, but when she went into them, he held her awkwardly, with his forearms crossed behind her. She pulled back. When she did, she saw the reason for his awkwardness.

She gasped, taking his wrists. She turned his hands over, revealing ugly blisters on several of his fingertips and an open blister on the heel of his right palm. The skin on most of his fingers was reddened. "You can't work at the dam like this," she said. "Your hands will get infected."

Lucas gestured toward the car. "I brought gloves," he said.

Rosamar said, "Vernettie's given him some salve, too." Wrinkling her nose, she walked closer, as if she realized that the private moment between Lucas and Ashley was over and that it was okay to approach them. "I'm surprised you can't smell it."

Thunder rumbled above them, plunging Ashley back into the atmosphere of her dreams. She looked up, remembering that moment when she had lain on the ground staring wet-eyed at the fast-moving clouds that darkened the sky. She felt as helpless now as she had in that moment. Refusing to look had weakened her, perhaps with fatal consequences for Nikki.

She lowered her gaze to the trees on the other side of the drive, but her vision was blurred. Her tears transformed the woods into smears of green and brown in which no single tree was distinct from the others.

"We'd better get to work," Clay said, glancing up at the sky and then turning toward Ashley and Lucas. "We're going to have a hard time keeping our footing on those stones once this storm hits and water starts rushing through the channel."

"Not yet," Ashley said. She shuddered as if a chill wind had blown against her back.

Clay watched her from under his eyebrows. Lucas

145

and Rosamar watched her as well. Ashley put her hands to her neck and felt nothing, but she thought that her friends must see what she could not: her own fear taking flesh, snaking around her neck, strangling her. "We can't go yet," she croaked. "I have to tell you about what I remember of one of my dreams. It had something to do with Nikki, and I didn't write it down. If something happens to me in the woods today, you have to be able to tell Vernettie. She's the only other person who might be able to interpret it."

"What do you think is going to happen to you?" Lucas asked.

Ashley swallowed, and felt against the constriction in her throat. "I don't know," she said. "I don't know."

Leaning against the car for support, with the others ranged in a semi-circle facing her, Ashley told them about her dream of Grandmother Birdie. When she had finished, there was a silence, and then Lucas asked, "Will everything happen exactly the way it did in the dream?"

"Maybe not, according to what Vernettie told me," she said. "She said that the dreams are like omens. Or prophecies."

Rosamar bunched her lips. "We don't have to consult Vernettie to find out whether that dream was a bad omen or not," she said.

Ashley had thought that sharing the dream with the others would ease the terrible sense of helplessness that had gripped her since she had awakened, but it hadn't. Pushing away from the car, she went to stand near Lucas. He held an arm out, and she slipped under it, leaning her head on his shoulder.

Clay took off his cap and hit it against his knee. "I don't like that snake business," he said. "Especially after what happened the other day. We'll have to be on the watch today."

Something about what Clay had said reminded Ashley of her second dream, the one where the snake had struck Charnas in the throat. Twice in one night, she had woken herself without allowing a dream to unroll its secrets, and now she found herself wondering what had happened to the young man.

Clay put his cap back on, then started walking away from the group, toward the storage building in the back, but stopped when he had walked about halfway. "Grandmother Birdie said something in the dream about a lake of fire?" he asked.

Ashley nodded.

"The closest lake is Lake Conroe, and you said that . . . demon, or whatever you call him, stays pretty close to this place," he said.

Again Ashley nodded.

"So I'm confused about what the lake of fire could mean," Clay said. "Do you think that you dreamed about fire because of the fire we set yesterday? Because it was on your mind?"

"I don't know," Ashley said. "It's possible."

Clay turned to Lucas. "I was just thinking. What do you think it would take to set a lake on fire?" he asked.

"I don't know," Lucas said. "Something flammable that would float on the surface. Gasoline, maybe. Lighter fluid. Why?"

"Nothing," Clay said. His eyebrows were drawn together in thought, but then he shook his head and said, "I'm going to get the tools."

Lucas started after him, but Rosamar stopped him.

"No, you stay with Ashley," she said. "I'll help Clay." She raised her eyebrows and stared at Lucas until he smiled.

"Besides," she said. "We might as well save your hands as long as possible." Turning to Ashley, she asked, "What about water and stuff for us to drink?"

"I packed a basket. I'll get it."

Rosamar waved her hand. "Clay and I will get it."

Lucas came back to Ashley. They stood close together, but didn't talk while the others were gone. Ashley looked at his dark brown hair and crooked eyebrow and then down at his burned hands. She remembered wishing once that he were as mysterious as Charnas, but that wish seemed childish now. She no longer thought of Lucas's steadiness and loyalty as uninteresting. They were the qualities that calmed her enough so that she could fight for Nikki's life.

Rosamar and Clay returned a few minutes later. In addition to the tools that Clay carried, Rosamar had located the picnic basket. A squarish object about the size of a large dictionary and wrapped in a chamois had been added to the contents of the basket.

"What's that?" Ashley asked.

Clay's face reddened and he coughed. Ashley saw Rosamar glance at Lucas with a quick look, but then she shrugged. "We just added some extra stuff to the picnic supplies," she said. "I didn't think that you would mind." She moved the picnic basket to the other hand, then looked up at the sky. "Whatever's going to happen is going to happen today, isn't it?"

"Yes, I'm afraid so," Ashley said, turning to gaze in the direction in which the dam lay.

Three hours later, she was still afraid, even though the morning's work had been uneventful. Leaning

148

with her back propped against a rough-barked pine, she watched as Lucas peeled off one of the gloves he had worn all morning. Several of the blisters on his fingers had opened and were weeping a thin, clear liquid.

Ashley winced and looked back at the dam. The point of the notched channel now reached within a few stone's height of the top of the pond. "Once we knock out those last stones," she asked, "how quickly will the creek flood?"

Lucas wiped the sweat from his forehead, then grimaced and lowered his hands, shaking them. "Depends," he said. "Close to the dam, it's going to flood pretty quickly, but there's a lot of dry bed to cover and the opening is narrow. Unless it rains hard, it may take a few hours before the water can do more than wet the soil."

Clay followed Rosamar as she started across the dam. A mockingbird darted down, arrowing straight toward Clay's head. He ducked, taking off his cap to swat at the bird.

"We need that rain," Lucas said, glancing at Clay's efforts to drive the bird away, but not smiling as he would have done any other time.

Something in his voice caught Ashley's attention. She walked to the edge of the bank and looked down, not caring if the mockingbird chose to attack her. "This whole arm of the creek will still flood even if it doesn't rain, won't it?" she asked.

Rosamar and Clay made it across the dam, Clay flapping his cap and muttering under his breath as he and Rosamar ran under the shelter of the nearest trees. There had been a harmony between all four of them all day, as if each were treasuring the time they were spending together. Still, there was an undercurrent of sadness to everything they did. Ashley thought it must be like the feeling among friends when one of them was dying.

She heard Lucas moving toward her, walking across the springy grass that grew near the bank. "It will still flood?" she asked again, without looking at him.

"Yes," he said, "but Clay and I have been talking. It looks as if this arm of the creek sits higher than the other part. Maybe water only runs through here whenever there's enough runoff."

"So you're saying that the water won't stay?" Ashley asked.

"I think that water will run through this part of the creek for a while, maybe even a long while. It's hard to tell. You said there were dead fish in there just after the dam was built. Maybe this part of the creek held water for a year or two at a time, but I don't think it always did. Not during dry spells. Like you said the other day, we may be just buying a little time until we find another way to keep the demon away."

Thunder rumbled above them, sounding as if a flexible sheet of metal had been shaken. Ashley walked along the bank to the dam, listening to the high, keening sound inside her head. Down from the dam, the pond was cloudy with dirt and debris that had fallen while they were working. She imagined the surface frothy and swirling with currents, a whirlpool forming as the water rushed through the narrow channel. She looked across to the opposite bank, where Grandmother Birdie had stood in her dreams, and it was as if she were hearing the old woman speak to her now. *And your covenant with death shall be disannulled, and your agreement with hell shall not stand; when the overflowing scourge shall pass through, then ye shall be trodden down by it.* Ashley's thoughts rushed forward toward that one limiting factor—that the creek must remain flooded—and then her imagination broke through onto the other side.

"Lucas!" she said, her voice so low that she wasn't sure that he would hear her.

When she turned, he was watching her, his eyebrow raised. He took one look at her, then came over immediately. "What is it?" he asked.

"Remember that part from my first dream about something overflowing?" she asked.

"I remember," he said.

She looked up into his face. He was beginning to smile, and she wondered why, but then she realized that she was smiling, too, and that he must be responding to her.

Clay and Rosamar must have noticed that something was going on. They came over, walking close to each other, but not touching. "The quote didn't say anything about standing water," Ashley said, including them. "It was about water overflowing and passing through!"

"What's going on?" Clay asked. He wiped his face with his forearm. His cheeks were reddened by his exertions.

"I think I know how to interpret one of my dreams!" Ashley said. "Maybe water doesn't have to stand on this side all the time. I think it's the actual flooding of this arm of the creek that's important."

As she talked, Lucas stepped away from her, stopping at the edge of the bank and squatting down, looking along the length of the creek. Ashley glanced

151

at him, but then Clay spoke, drawing her attention to him.

"Don't go so fast!" he said. "There's something I don't understand. After you found out about that other baby back at the cabin, you told us that the only reason that the demon kept away from her so long was that the water that circled the property kept him from getting to this side of the creek. Now you say it's a flood that will keep him away. It couldn't have been in the act of flooding all the time that she was alive. She was what, a year old?"

Watching Ashley's face, Rosamar said, "Maybe Ashley's not talking about just keeping him away?" She took Ashley's hands in her own. "You're talking about stopping him for good, aren't you?"

"Killing him?" Clay asked. "You mean killing him?"

Ashley looked away, past Rosamar's shoulder. She hadn't thought about it that way, but she guessed that was what she meant. Her fingers felt cold against Rosamar's warm hands. She remembered the stench of the demon, the rotten look of his flesh. "I'm not sure that he's alive," she said.

"Well, if he's already dead, then we'll kill him a second time!" Clay said.

Ashley nodded, but her sense of celebration was blunted by Lucas's continued absorption in the creek. She sensed something wrong. Leaving the others, she walked to where he knelt. She put her hand on his shoulder. He lifted his hand as if to place it over hers, then opened his injured fingers and lowered his hand. "There's a problem," he said.

A muscle under Ashley's ribcage spasmed, as if warning her to prepare for something that she didn't want to hear.

152

"If the flood's supposed to kill him," Lucas said, "then doesn't he have to be in the creek itself when the dam breaks? How are we going to get him in the creek, Ash?"

Covering her mouth with her hand, Ashley turned away from him. She stared at Rosamar, whose T-shirt was stained orange from the red dirt that had clung to the stones. Rosamar's eyes gradually widened.

"Oh, please, no," Rosamar whispered. "That's what you were supposed to see in the dream, wasn't it? When Nikki was in the water? What was it Grandmother Birdie said for you to look at, exactly?"

Ashley's lips were cold and stiff. "She said for me to look at Nikki. She said that *Nikki* had drawn him to her."

SEVENTEEN

No one said anything for a long moment. Ashley tried not to cry, but tears streamed down her face and her nose stopped up. She was aware of the others standing near her, but she didn't look at them. She didn't want to see the expressions on their faces.

"We have to use Nikki to lure the demon down there," she said. Her voice was thick and sounded flat and comical inside her head. The humid air seemed to press against the bones of her face.

"There has to be another way," Rosamar said.

"There isn't," Ashley said. "I think I must have known that all along. I just didn't want to accept it." She looked at Rosamar, then quickly back down at the bed of the creek. Dried and decayed leaves lined the ground. If the flooding of the creek were swift enough, the water would scour out the bed, cleansing it of all of the debris that lined it now. She wished that she could lie down there and be washed away along with the leaves.

"I've got an idea," Clay said. "We could fool him somehow. Make him think that Nicole is down there. Use some of her clothes or something for scent."

Ashley shook her head without looking at him.

"He's not a dog, Clay," she said. "Besides, for all we know, he's hearing everything we're talking about this minute. Or maybe he can read my mind. We don't know what powers he has."

Lucas spoke. "If we bring Nicole back here and he knows all the time that we're trying to trap him, will he even go down there after her?"

Ashley sniffed back her tears. "If he wants her badly enough. And I think that he does."

"So it would come down to whether we could time everything well enough," Lucas said. "We would have to flood the creek right at the moment he tried to get to Nicole."

"What do you think that the water will do to him?" Rosamar asked. "Does he *melt?*"

As frightened as Ashley was at the moment, she felt the corners of her mouth turning up in a smile. "I seriously doubt it," she said. She took in a long, shivery breath. "In the dream last night, there was a sort of religious feel to everything that happened. And Grandmother Birdie wasn't just saying what she said, she was chanting it. Like a ritual of some kind." She stopped, suddenly remembering the other dream, when someone else, the one-armed man, had also chanted.

"So the water is part of the ritual?" Clay asked.

Ashley lifted her shoulders without answering. "You know," she said, "when Grandmother Birdie told me to look, she didn't sound horrified. She sounded as if she were gloating. As if she'd won something." She looked at Rosamar. "Maybe it's going to turn out all right."

"I don't know," Rosamar said. "I say we flood the creek the way we planned and just keep him on the other side. Let some other generation deal with him.''

Some other generation. For an instant, the idea was tempting to Ashley. Her dreams might be troubled with the death of a baby not yet born, but it was Nikki she cared most about. ''But what if the water recedes next winter, or the winter after that? We have no idea how old Nikki has to be before he lets her alone.''

Clay walked up and stood next to Rosamar. His face looked thin and drawn, and his mouth turned down at the corners. He put his hand on Rosamar's shoulder. Rosamar looked up at him, and then, when she saw his face, she turned to face him and took his hand. He gazed at Rosamar for a moment, then turned to look at Ashley. ''There's only one way to be sure that he doesn't come back after Nicole, isn't there, and that's to destroy him completely. It's crazy, but we have to risk her life in order to save it, don't we?''

Ashley nodded. Then she bit her lip to keep it from trembling and looked down at the leaves strewn on the bed of the creek.

The first drops of rain slanted toward the ground an hour later. Before Ashley and the others had time to react, a clap of thunder sounded, signaling a harder rain that drilled into the ground, kicking up puffs of red, sandy soil. Ashley pushed back her dripping bangs and watched a rivulet of water zigzag down the slope of the bank toward the creek.

She turned toward Lucas and Clay. Rosamar had headed back to the house thirty minutes earlier in order to call Vernettie and tell her what had been decided. Now it was time for Ashley to go back, so that she would be there waiting when Vernettie and Nikki arrived. Lucas and Clay would remain behind to prepare for the removal of the last stones.

Ashley lowered her head as the sobs overcame her again, as they had several times in this last hour. Lucas slogged through the rain toward her. He offered his hand. Ashley took it, feeling the raw places on his palm against her own palm, the broken flesh beneath her fingers.

Clay crossed from the dam to the bank. He hesitated, watching them, then trudged over to join them. He wiped his hands, grimy from the work and wet from the rain, and then took Ashley's hand and Lucas's.

They were all united, hand to hand. To Ashley, the circle they completed seemed a part of the strange sense of ceremony and ritual which had marked this day.

"It's time," she said, letting go of Clay's hand.

Lucas wouldn't release her. Rain washed between their clasped hands. "Let me go," she whispered to him.

He shook his head. "Not alone," he said. "Rosie was safe enough. If the demon knew what we were planning, he would have wanted her to make it back to the house and call Vernettie. It was the only way he could get Nikki back here. But he'll want to stop you."

Ashley leaned her forehead against Lucas's shoulder. "If anything happens to me, will you take Nikki down to the creek?" she asked, looking up at him.

He shook his head. Droplets of water fell from the ends of his hair onto Ashley's nose and cheeks. "Not without you to tell us what to do."

"Then I'm safe for the time being. He needs me,

too." She sighed and wiped the rain from her eyes with one hand. "After you've signaled us that you're breaking out the last of the stones, Rosamar will come find you. She'll bring you to where we've left Nikki."

Lucas squeezed her hand and then let her go. She felt his concerned gaze on her until she had slipped through the trees and out of his line of vision, but then she was alone with her fear and misgivings. The woods were dark and lashed by rain. She pushed herself to move faster and faster, even after her lungs began to burn and her breath to come short and quick.

When she finally broke out into the open, she stopped, her hands on her chest. She stared up at the house, struck anew by the stark lines of the stuccoed walls. Even though she knew the house to be less than eleven years old, it looked solid enough to have stood there for decades, for centuries, as if it might even have been constructed in those days when the demon had walked the earth as a living man.

Ashley saw the front door opening, as she had known that it would. She had already spotted Vernettie's truck parked under the protective overhang of an oak. She started forward, her legs heavy with fatigue, a stitch in her side, her throat and lungs burning.

Rosamar walked outside first, but Vernettie waited in the open doorway. She held Nikki, who was bundled in something yellow. Vernettie's dampened hair frizzed about her face. Her skirt was limp and clung to her thin legs.

As Ashley crossed the driveway and drew near, Vernettie's eyes caught her attention. They were red, the skin around them puffy. Ashley stopped, her fear so physical a thing that it blocked her breathing and kept her from moving. "You've been crying!" she said. She glanced over her shoulder at Rosamar, but Rosamar was looking away so that she only saw the back of her head.

"Take her," Vernettie said.

Ashley turned back. Nikki was bundled in their father's yellow rain slicker. It was folded about her in such a way that only her eyes and nose and mouth were visible. Her eyes moved back and forth, then focused on Ashley's face.

Wiping away the rain that dripped from the tip of her nose, Ashley turned away from her sister's gaze to look down the length of the driveway to where it curved, just before dipping down toward the old creek bed. Then she turned and held out her arms.

Horror rang through her bones as Nikki's weight settled into her arms. She looked down at her sister's sweet face and then looked up at Vernettie. "I can't," she said, her voice hoarse and thick. "I can't go through with this."

Vernettie backed up, drawing the door closed behind her smoothly and quickly. When Ashley realized what she was doing, she leaped for the door, hunching protectively over Nikki. The dead bolt slid into place just as Ashley's shoulder hit the door.

They were locked outside.

Ashley whirled, her back to the door. Water squished inside her shoes.

Rosamar stood with her fingers over her mouth, her lips mashed against her teeth.

Ashley heard something tapping behind her. She turned and found that Vernettie stood in the side window. Ashley leaned her forehead against the glass, too grief-stricken even to cry. A wind rose behind her, howling toward the house, carrying rain and debris with it. To Ashley, hunching over Nikki protectively, it sounded as if the world were ending.

From the other side of the glass, Vernettie put one hand near Nikki's head and the other near Ashley's in a gesture of benediction or farewell. She held her hands there for a moment, as the sudden gust of wind died and the world quieted, and then she turned and walked away through the dim foyer and into the darker hallway that led to the kitchen.

"No!" Ashley screamed. She shifted Nikki so that she could hold her in one arm. With the other hand, she pounded on the window.

"Come back!" she screamed, her throat raw with the force of her screaming. She pounded until she was afraid that the window would shatter, then she moved to the door and she pounded on that.

Rosamar pulled her away from the door, grabbing her wrist and twisting her arm up to show her that the side of her hand was bloodied.

Her blood was smeared on the door, too. Ashley stared at it, remembering the ceremonial feel to this day. Suddenly it seemed to her that the bloodletting was a necessary part of the ritual. It seemed as if all of this had been foreordained, even her own attempt to back out at the last moment.

Nikki's hands moved beneath the protective covering of the raingear, as if she were reaching for a strand of Ashley's hair. Ashley cupped the side of Nikki's face with her hand. She felt Nikki's skin warm beneath her own cold, cold fingers. She drew in a deep breath, smelling the wet ground and the cedar and the sweet milkiness of her sister's breath.

Then she wiped the side of her hand across Nikki's forehead, smearing blood there.

Rosamar grabbed her hand. "What are you doing?" she asked, her voice low and far back in her throat. Her expression was fierce.

"It's a sign of my protection," Ashley said. "For the demon." She turned and started down the flagstone walk. Nikki blinked and arched her back as the first raindrops hit her face.

Rosamar ran in front of Ashley and stopped her. She grabbed Ashley's upper arm just above the elbow and squeezed so tightly that Ashley winced. "Are you sure you know what you're doing?" she asked, staring with narrowed eyes into Ashley's eyes.

Looking over Rosamar's shoulder, into the woods on the near side of the drive, Ashley saw a dark shape that crossed an open space in a manner that no shadow should have done. She drew in a sharp breath. "I'd better," she said. "I'd better know exactly what I'm doing."

EIGHTEEN

"*He's out* there now," Ashley whispered to Rosamar.

Rosamar turned to look over her shoulder. There was no reason to whisper, Ashley realized, but she had a dread of Nikki hearing what they were saying. Nikki had always seemed to her to be more observant than other babies. More wise. She knew that Nikki couldn't really understand what she was saying, but she still couldn't bring herself to speak out loud.

"We'll go down the driveway to where it crosses the dry bed of the creek," she continued. "If he's really afraid of the water, then I don't think he'll risk going down into the creek unless Nikki is alone. There should be some runoff down there already. If he's been watching us, he'll know how close we are to breaking through the dam."

Rosamar moved to Ashley's side as if to shield Nikki. They walked together, Rosamar matching her stride to Ashley's. Water stood in pools on the oily surface of the drive. Occasional raindrops fell, but the rain was slowing to a drizzle.

Nikki had been silent until now, but she squirmed in Ashley's arms and let out a sharp cry. Ashley shifted her against her shoulder so that the rain wouldn't fall on her face.

"Don't let her make any noise," Rosamar said. She turned to look behind them, then gasped.

Ashley hesitated, missing a step, but then she moved ahead again without looking back. She knew what Rosamar must have seen. "We want him to follow us," she said, her voice gentle, crooning almost. She could feel the tension gathering in her little sister's body and wanted to soothe her.

The driveway followed the gentle slope of the bank, crossing the dry arm of the creek at its highest point.

"Ashley, I can't see him any more," Rosamar said. "I don't know how close he is."

Nodding, Ashley turned to the right, leaving the asphalted drive. Rosamar followed. Immediately, they found it harder making way. The decaying vegetation was slick, and the wet clay beneath that even more slick. Ashley stopped to reposition Nikki.

"Don't stop," Rosamar said, putting her hand on Ashley's right elbow. Her voice was low, carrying such a note of strain that Ashley started, looking to see what had frightened her.

The demon was on the low bank near them, his height augmented by their position below him.

One leap, and he could be on them.

The rain must have masked his smell, but Ashley's throat closed with a remembered reflex. She glared at him, holding Nikki's head tight against her shoulder.

He opened his mouth, a dark socket to match the sockets of his eyes, showing her a stump that could only be what was left of his tongue. Ashley shuddered. Whatever horrible bargain he had made in order to cheat his death, he had lost the power of speech. She thought his silence more frightening than any speech might have been.

"Go," Rosamar said, pushing her. Rosamar's hair was sleek against her head. She looked grim and powerful. Without makeup, her features revealed their ancient casting. She looked like more like a priestess, a seer, than did Ashley. She seemed a more fitting participant in what was happening. For a moment, Ashley considered handing Nikki over to her.

They splashed through the water, urging each other forward. When water sloshed in Ashley's shoes and over her ankles, she realized that the water level was rising. Water must have begun streaming through the lowest part of the channel. She prayed that Lucas and Clay wouldn't break out the last of the stones too soon. The demon must be in the channel at the time that it flooded.

The path of the creek curved northward. Water parted to either side of a large sandstone slab with an almost flat top. To Ashley, it looked eerie sitting there, and then she realized that it resembled an altar. She paused near it, thinking that it might be high enough and wide enough to protect Nikki from the rising water, but then she glanced up and saw the demon watching her. She felt the current of knowledge that passed between them. If she knew that the slab looked like an altar, then he must know it, too. She started walking again.

Up ahead, the creek turned, with the ground sloping downward. The bank rose nearly vertically to a height two or three feet over Ashley's head. She glanced up to confirm that the demon still followed them. When she looked at Nikki again, she saw that the yellow slicker had fallen away from her face.

Nikki held herself still, her eyes opened wide and turned up to focus on the demon. She stared at him, her soft lips puckered as if she were about to cry.

164

He watched her, head down, breath wheezing in and out of the ragged openings in his chest and throat. Ashley felt as if the rain had somehow found its way into her heart, chilling her blood, chilling her hands and feet as the blood traveled to them.

Hurrying out into the center of the dry bed, Ashley repositioned Nikki on her shoulder, pulling the slicker up again. Never had she felt such hatred. She hadn't known it was possible. It tore at her heart and her stomach, filling her with a cold rage that left no room for thinking. She wanted to scream and scream her anger, but that would only frighten Nikki more.

"Listen," Rosamar said, pulling her to a stop. "Do you hear that sound? It's Lucas and Clay. They're signaling us that they're ready to push out the last stones."

Listening, Ashley heard the signal: a rhythmic clanging of sledgehammer against stone. The sound seemed of a piece with the time in which the trees of these woods were first seeded, in which the demon first lived and died and made his agreement with hell. Grief, thicker and more harsh than blood, coursed through Ashley's veins.

It was time.

Time to find as secure a place as possible to leave Nikki. Time to walk away from her, taunting the demon with the possibility of having her.

Rosamar turned. Ashley noted that her cheeks seemed almost hollow beneath the broad, prominent planes of her cheekbones. Ashley looked into her deep-set eyes for a long moment, and then Rosamar broke the gaze. She sloshed forward again, heading toward a turn to the right. Ashley trudged after her, searching as she went for a secure place in which to leave Nikki. She looked for a hollowed-out spot high on the wall of the bank or a high place in the center of the bed of the creek, but she saw nothing suitable. An artery in her neck began to throb as she moved with increasing urgency. There could only be a few minutes left before the rush of water would be on them.

Overhead, black clouds rolled over even darker clouds, obscuring the sun's light. As Ashley walked forward, she moved through the sunless and wet air. Heavy, wind-driven drops of rain began to fall.

As she neared the turn in the creek, she tried not to think of anything but the immediate task at hand. Out in the middle of the stream, and almost beyond the turn now, Rosamar stopped, waiting for Ashley to catch up. The rain came down harder, splashing in the rising water. Through a break in the sheeting rain, Ashley saw Rosamar shield her eyes to look in her direction and then raise her gaze. Rosamar's hands fell away from her eyes.

With a cold sinking in her stomach, Ashley turned and saw what had frightened Rosamar.

Above the point where Ashley stood, the bank jutted toward the center of the stream. A tree grew near the overhang, its branches stretching nearly to the opposite side. The demon stood beneath that tree. Ashley might almost have reached up and touched his feet.

Trying to blink away the raindrops that fell on her lashes, Ashley stared up at him. The rain had wet his skin, the moisture giving it a reflective quality that it had lacked on other occasions. His skin had absorbed the water unevenly, taking on a ribbed and bumpy texture. The split flesh around his mouth and on his chest had reddened. It looked pulpy. His nearly lidless eyes stared at her. A sinking terror turned her stomach cold and sapped the strength from her muscles. Quickly, she averted her gaze, afraid to look into his eyes any longer.

As soon as she started forward, she felt the water's resistance to her movements. "It's risen, hasn't it?" she called out to Rosamar.

From out in the creek, Rosamar nodded. Her mouth was set and her eyebrows drawn low. She gestured toward the part of the creek that Ashley couldn't see, beyond the turn. "There's no safe place for her as far as I can see in this direction," she said. "You'll have to go back to that big rock."

Ashley nodded. She had instinctively recognized the sandstone slab's suitability when she had seen it, how perfectly formed it seemed for the function she intended it to have. Its flat surface was wide enough to ensure that Nikki would not easily roll into the water, and it rose high out of the water, but she had been strangely reluctant to leave Nikki there. Part of that reluctance came from her conviction that the demon had sensed the slab's perfection, too, but only part.

"Get Lucas and Clay," she said to Rosamar. "Tell them where Nikki and I are."

Ashley wasn't sure how much their presence could help. From this point on, she sensed that the struggle to save Nikki would depend on an accurate interpretation of her dreams and not on anyone's physical strength.

Without arguing, Rosamar walked around the turn, not even shielding her eyes from the rain. Ashley's last glimpse of her was in profile: the wide planes of her cheekbones, the upright posture earned by years of gymnastics workouts.

Ashley and Nikki were alone with the demon. Ashley didn't look at him, but listened for the clanging sounds from the direction of the dam. And heard none.

Lucas and Clay had breached the dam, then. All that they could do had been done. The rest was up to her.

She waited through the space of several slow heartbeats, knowing what she would have to do next, but unable to move. Then she felt the water cold against her shin and realized that it was rising steadily.

But something was terribly wrong. Ashley remembered her dream, when the water had foamed and sprayed between the banks as it swept down the length of the creek. She remembered the words of Grandmother Birdie. *And your covenant with death shall be disannulled, and your agreement with hell shall not stand; when the overflowing scourge shall pass through, then ye shall be trodden down by it.*

This slow and steady rising of the water didn't match the image from her dream. It didn't seem to fulfill the prophecy in the words Grandmother Birdie had quoted. Ashley took several steps in the direction that Rosamar had gone. "Rosamar!" she called.

There was no answer. Ashley stopped to listen, but heard nothing but the rumble of thunder overhead and the roar of hard rain hitting the leaves and the surface of the water. She took several more steps forward and then stopped again. "This is wrong," she said to herself. "We've made a mistake. I've got to go back to the house."

She turned, glancing up at the bank, but that one glance was enough to stop her again.

She couldn't go back. Going back would be useless now. Looking up, she had realized something that she hadn't noticed earlier.

The demon had chosen to follow her along the bank that was nearest the house.

If he couldn't cross water, then once the flooding was completed, he would be trapped *inside* the circle formed by the two arms of the creek. Inside the circle, where the house stood.

Ashley looked down at her little sister. She had quieted a few minutes earlier, her body melting against Ashley's. When Ashley pulled back the yellow slicker to see Nikki's face better, she saw that her little sister had fallen asleep. Her long, brownish-blond lashes lay on her cheek.

Standing in the middle of the stream, looking down at her sister, Ashley felt the cold rain hitting her back, and she acknowledged the horrible truth. Going back to the house now meant resigning herself to Nikki's eventual death at the demon's hands.

Their only weapon against him was the dream-knowledge granted to her. No matter how hopeless the effort might seem now, Nikki's only hope lay in carrying out the plan that Ashley and the others had devised.

But if there was to be no rush of water, then she might take the time to grieve. She closed her eyes, then tilted her face up to the sky and let the rain wash away her tears. The keening noise was back in her ears, ringing through her head, sounding a death toll. Ashley wanted to scream out her fear and grief, but she kept silent so that Nikki might sleep.

Then she slogged back to the sandstone slab. The current pushed against the backs of her legs, urging her to move faster while she longed to postpone the moment that must come.

When she reached the slab, the rising water already lapped within inches of its top surface. Gingerly, Ashley lowered Nikki to the slab.

Rain hit Nikki's face. Ashley thought that she might wake then, but her head lolled back, her limbs relaxed under the slicker. Rain and perspiration had soaked her hair, so that it curled next to her scalp in separate tendrils. Ashley longed to touch her cheek and wake her so that she might look into her eyes once more. She wanted to speak words of apology that Nikki wouldn't even understand. Instead, she clenched her hands into fists. Whatever happened in these next moments, she prayed that Nikki would sleep through it. That if Nikki were to suffer death at the demon's hands, she would be spared the fear, at least.

Over the sound of the lashing rain and the wind in the trees, Ashley heard a thin, helpless moaning coming from the direction of the bank. Thinking that it might be Rosamar or one of the guys, she whirled to face the bank.

It was the demon making the noise. He watched her as he did it, his head back, his ruined throat vibrating.

He was moaning for Nikki. The sound was obscene, horrible in its weakness and hunger. Acid hatred burned through Ashley's veins.

She covered her ears, but still she could hear it. To drown out the sound, she tried to whisper a prayer. The only words that came to her were the words from the prophecy in her dream. She chanted them as if they were a curse or an incantation. She sang them as if they were a lullaby to her sister, to ease her sleeping.

And the demon's moaning changed, deepening

into a bellow that shuddered the air and made Ashley take a step backward in alarm. Recovering, she chanted louder, as if the words were a part of a rite of exorcism to be directed against him.

The demon roared. Knowing that she had angered him, Ashley knew her power over him. She smiled a smile that was almost a grimace, her lips drawn back over her teeth. She was a dreamer, and these were the words that the dream had given her, and she saw now that they had power.

The demon was fear incarnate. The dreams and the dream-knowledge were the weapons with which she armed herself and Nikki against him.

But first she must believe in her dreams and trust the knowledge that she gleaned there, and then she must act to make the dreams come true.

Now that she believed, the time had come to act.

With one last look at her sister, Ashley staggered upstream, away from Nikki, in the direction in which Rosamar had gone. She planned to go just far enough so that the demon would be tempted to go into the water.

She had to do this, she told herself. She had to surrender her sister in the hope of saving her. Still, grief bowed her down so that she bent double, the ends of her hair falling into the water.

NINETEEN

Still stooped forward, Ashley rounded the turn in the creek's bed and then stopped. She would not go a step farther away from Nikki. Her stomach heaving, she covered her mouth with her hands.

Then, even before she could turn back to watch for the demon's first move, Nikki cried out. Her cry was thin, sharp, startled.

Ashley whirled around. With rough motions, she wiped tears and rain from her lashes and eyes. The spot where the tree stood on the bank was high and visible for a distance. Even from beyond the turn, even through the gloom and the rain, she should have been able to spot the demon beneath the branches of the tree.

He was gone.

The noise of the storm must have masked the awful clacking of his bones as he had entered the water.

Slogging through the knee-deep water, Ashley started back toward the turn in the creek. Her heart knocked against the inside of her chest as she tried to push through the water more quickly. She had misjudged how far to go and how long to leave Nikki unattended. Her temples pounded with sudden pain.

Then, before Ashley reached the turn, before she had taken more than three or four steps, a chocolate-brown cottonmouth swam out from behind the bend.

Contrary to what she believed about a snake's habits, it swam upstream, directly toward her.

She jerked to a stop. The snake swam with whipping motions, moving quickly. She tried to back up and lost her balance, falling into the water. Landing heavily on her right buttock and side, her head went underwater. She tasted the warm, brackish water and realized that this taste, this sensation, might be her last.

But if she died, then there would be no one to save Nikki.

With her arms flailing to keep her balance, Ashley scrambled into a sitting position, facing toward the turn, blinking frantically to clear her eyes so that she could see.

The snake swam several feet closer, its body rippling with the movement. Watching it, breathing through her open mouth, Ashley scooted back against the current.

The snake seemed to watch her, too, its head pointed toward her as its body whipped back and forth with its swimming motions.

Her thoughts were fragmented, flashing through her mind. She considered lying flat on the bottom until the snake swam past.

Then, before she could act, a second snake slipped from the bank, twisting in the air as it fell, splashing into the water only a few feet away from where she sat.

At the same moment, Nikki's cries rose in pitch.

They were joined by another sound—a cry so full

of horrid joy that, hearing it, Ashley covered her ears with her hands.

"No!" she roared, finding her voice. She pushed to her feet.

The second snake swam so close that Ashley could see the black transverse markings on its body, the white on the inside of its mouth. She was plunged back into the last night's dream, when the snakes had crawled around her neck. Remembering, her throat muscles tightened, nearly closing off her windpipe. For a moment, it seemed that she couldn't breathe. She scrambled backwards, her shoes sliding on the muck underfoot.

Then she remembered that she had been the one who had pulled the vines across her face. Out of her own fear, she had precipitated that part of the dream. Now that same fear was making her more vulnerable than she might be. She knew better than to try to outrun a snake. She knew what to do.

The muscles in Ashley's legs quivered with the need to run, but she forced herself to stand still.

The snake swam past her, its body undulating, its muscled flesh touching her calf. The entire surface of her skin quivered, and her teeth chattered, but she managed not to move her feet.

There was still another snake to threaten her, and now it approached.

Frantic, she glanced from the snake to the turn in the creek. Suddenly, she understood the demon's purpose in sending the snakes to threaten her.

He had Nikki. Now he wanted time alone with her, without Ashley nearby. But only a little time.

The snakes that threatened her now were sent to give him that time.

Brightly colored spots circled and spiralled through

Ashley's vision, as if it were her mouth that the demon was covering with his own, her breath that he was stealing. She staggered forward, trying to keep her balance. She would have to get past the other snake quickly. Even if it were to bite her, she reasoned that she would have time enough to reach Nikki before the poison began to act.

As she moved, one of her shoes stuck in the mud, slipping from her foot.

The snake changed its course to match her change in position, angling toward her. Then, farther out in the stream, Ashley glimpsed movement. A third snake swam there, its head lifted above the surface of the water.

Think, she told herself. *You'll know what to do if you just think about it.*

Reaching down, Ashley fished through the muddied water for her shoe, watching the progress of the snakes. Bent over, her face near the surface of the water, she watched until the first one was close enough that she was sure of her aim. Pulling the shoe free from the mud, she tossed it, hitting the snake in the middle of its body.

It wrapped its long, sinuous body around the shoe, plunging its head toward the canvas, closing its jaws. The other snake darted forward, striking the shoe.

Ashley ran past the snakes, around the turn in the creek.

And stopped, throwing her hands out to the side for balance.

The water now lapped the top of the sandstone slab. Nikki seemed to float in the middle of the stream, just as she had in the dream. Water eddied around the slab, parting to either side.

Nikki lay rigid, her head and neck arched and her

legs extended beneath the slicker. The demon crouched over her.

Ashley must have made some sound, because he turned to look at her. His roar of exultation rose, his wounded throat vibrating obscenely. Water that was contaminated with his shredding skin washed over Nikki's face, then receded.

Ashley slogged forward, walking as if she were an automaton. A heavy dullness radiated out from the center of her chest. For a shocked moment, she thought that her heart might actually have stopped beating.

Nikki's mouth opened, her chest contracting as she coughed. She kicked, the slicker bulging outward at her feet.

Then, when Ashley was no more than half the distance between the turn in the creek and Nikki, the demon reached forward and lifted her from the slab.

Ashley's lips went cold. The demon unwound the rain slicker from Nikki and tossed it into the water. Ashley forced herself to keep walking toward him.

The slicker floated away, snagging on the slab and then moving past. Ashley felt a calm descend over her even as Nikki screamed, her eyes squeezed shut and her mouth opened wide. The time for agonizing over decisions was past. There was some relief in knowing that she must act now, and act quickly, and that, afterwards, the trauma would be over in one way or another.

As she closed the distance between herself and the demon, she noted that the water splashed up high into the air as the strong current hit the slab. The water splashed Nikki, washing over the blood that Ashley had smeared on her forehead.

Instinct informed Ashley's actions. She seemed to

know what to do without thinking about it first. She reached out, and noted that both her hand and her arm trembled.

The demon watched without trying to stop her, his mossy teeth bared in a grimace. He let Ashley reach toward Nikki's forehead, as she had somehow known that he would.

Nikki stopped screaming, twisting to look up at Ashley's hand, her eyes crossing in the effort to focus.

Time seemed to stop as Ashley's hand made contact with Nikki's forehead. In that moment, the water and the blood formed a seal between them.

Ashley knew what to do now. She had seen how the incantation had affected the demon while he was still on the bank. Now she must repeat the words while he was in the water.

With her finger firmly pressed against Nikki's forehead, she began. "Your covenant with death shall be disannulled," she said, dipping her free hand into the floodwater.

The demon hissed. When Ashley looked down, she saw that the current was washing away bits of his flesh. Bile rose to the back of her throat, so that she could not speak for a moment, but then she continued. "Your agreement with hell shall not stand." She lifted her hand, water dripping from her fingertips.

Then, just as she was ready to complete the incantation, she saw movement out of the corner of her eye. With one hand still on Nikki's forehead and the other dripping water, she looked.

Lucas slipped over the edge of the bank, wading silently to a stop where Ashley could see him clearly. Clay followed, with the chamois-wrapped bundle tucked under his arm. Rosamar knelt on the bank, placing a small box on the ground next to her.

"Take Nicole now," Lucas said. His face was ashen beneath streaks of red dirt.

The world rushed back at Ashley, all the colors and scents and textures she had shut out. Her finger was still pressed against Nikki's forehead, but somehow the seal between them had weakened and the sense of ceremony was broken.

Ashley cried out. The demon curved his body over Nikki's, pushing Ashley's hand away.

Then, with Nikki in his arms, he turned, wading toward the opposite bank.

Lucas started after him, but Ashley shook her head and he stopped. She had to gain control again. The others were physically stronger than she, but it was her kind of strength that was needed now. She lifted her hand and noted the fresh drops of blood that welled up from the side of her fist. She would risk everything, including her own lifeblood. She would go with the demon into his lair, if that was necessary.

She started after him.

He reached the bank and laid the screaming baby dangerously close to the edge as he prepared to climb.

Drawing closer to him, Ashley bent over again, dipping both hands into the floodwater, cupping them to hold more water. "Demon!" she shouted.

Signaling with a shake of her head for Lucas and Clay to stay back, she slowly straightened, her cupped hands dripping water. She stepped forward, and began chanting. "All this will come to pass when the overflowing scourge shall pass through," she said.

178

When she finished, she flung the water at him.

The demon dropped from the bank. Surprised at the swiftness of his reaction and not knowing what to expect next, Ashley stood with hands upraised and mouth gaping open.

Regaining his feet, the demon rushed at her.

"Get out of the water!" Clay screamed. "Get out right now!"

Ashley crouched, too shocked to move. There were more words she had intended to speak, words from the other dream, but she couldn't remember them in the suddenness of this attack.

Then she was nearly jerked off her feet from behind. Gasping, she flailed. Lucas had hold of her arms. He dragged her toward the bank where Rosamar crouched. "Let me go," she pleaded, trying to break away. "I have to go to Nikki."

Despite the burns on his hands, Lucas tightened his grip on her arms. Ashley saw that the demon had stopped his rush toward her and had turned back toward the far bank.

Gathering her strength, Ashley threw herself forward, but Lucas swung her around to face the bank where Rosamar crouched forward, reaching for her. Losing her purchase on the slick bed of the creek, the current washed her feet out from under her.

With Rosamar's help, Lucas shoved Ashley onto the bank. She fell in a heap, her legs dangling off the edge of the bank. Rosamar had fallen backwards, but scrambled up and lay across Ashley, keeping her down on the ground while Lucas clambered up after her.

Lucas signaled Rosamar to back away. He took Ashley in his arms and held her against his chest. She lay with her cheek pressed against his chest and her face turned toward the creek, too stunned to cry. "There's something else to try," he said over and over, but Ashley hardly heard him. What else could be done? The water hadn't destroyed the demon. Even now, he was approaching the bank where Nikki lay. Once he reached her, once he escaped into the woods with her, then it would be too late to do anything.

But Lucas and the others were trying something, she saw. Clay stood in the middle of the creek, his feet planted wide for balance. He poured something out of a squarish can that he held, and then he tossed the can at the demon's back. He ran for the bank where Ashley and the others crouched. "Do it now, Rosamar!" he screamed. "Do it now! Don't wait for me to get out of the water!"

"What does he want us to do?" Ashley cried, watching Rosamar scoot forward and bend over something. "Tell me!" Ashley renewed her struggles when no one answered. "We have to get Nikki," she shouted.

Lucas was too strong for Ashley. His arms tightened around her. "Stay here," he yelled.

"No!" she screamed. She drew in a deep breath in order to scream again, but then she caught the distinctive odor of lighter fluid and the sharp smell of phosphorus.

Clay shouted, "Now!"

The sharp odors stung Ashley's nostrils, but so many things were happening at once that one sensation crowded out another. She saw and smelled and felt everything in vivid snatches of color and sound and odor and touch. Rosamar held a long kitchen match, already lighted. Clay ran toward them with his upper body leaning forward against the water's pull. He yelled, "Do it now before the current carries the lighter fluid too far downstream!"

Then Ashley realized what had been done and what was about to happen. Clay had poured an entire container of lighter fluid onto the surface of the water.

Rosamar leaned forward with the match in her hand. "No!" Ashley screamed. Lucas pulled her close to him, holding her head tight against his chest. "If he gets to Nikki, she'll burn to death with him!" she screamed against Lucas's chest.

Rosamar and Clay each yelled something, but Lucas's covering hand prevented Ashley from hearing what was said.

Then came the sound that Lucas's hand could not block out.

The water roared.

"Nikki!" Ashley screamed, flinging herself backward and breaking out of Lucas's grasp.

Blue flames spread across the water, hazing the air. The demon stood near the opposite bank, his body seeming to undulate in the haze.

Clay lay with his upper body across the bank as Rosamar tugged on his jeaned legs. Without rising, he rolled over, grabbing Ashley's ankle. "We did it!" he screamed. "We turned it into a lake of fire! He's burning up!"

Clay's eyes seem to have gone white with anger or frenzy. Frightened by his look, Ashley tried to kick his hand away. As she lunged backward, she looked across the water and then stopped fighting. A ray of sunlight had broken through the clouds, shining through the blue haze of the fire and spotlighting the sandstone slab in the middle of the stream.

Beyond the slab, nearer the bank, the demon burned.

Ashley gasped. As he burned, his body wicked up the water from the stream, expanding his tissues. For the first time, she and the others were seeing him as he had looked in life.

"It's over!" Clay yelled.

Ashley recognized the rounded forehead, the arched brows, the high cheekbones. She recognized him and she recognized this place.

He was Charnas and this was the place of magic. The sandstone slab was the stone where he had been placed.

"No!" Ashley screamed.

Clay released her ankle.

Lucas moved to the edge of the bank, then turned back to Ashley. "He's not dying, is he?" he yelled.

Mute, Ashley shook her head. She tried to think. The ceremony performed here had given Charnas an eternal life, but one earned by the horrible necessity to steal it from the most innocent. He wouldn't die, couldn't die, unless she could find a way to undo the magic.

Clay took one more look and then turned back to her. "Can you do anything?" he asked. His eyes were rimmed with red. The skin surrounding his mouth and nose was white.

Then, from somewhere inside herself, Ashley found the necessary calm, and memory, and knowledge. She remembered the dreams, and the knowledge she had gleaned, and the reaction of Charnas to the words of the first quote. The one-armed man had transformed him into something horrible, but Grandmother Birdie had given her the incantations to be used against him.

Drawing in a breath, she spoke. "Charnas!" she called. "I have come to give you back your name."

It seemed to her that her voice thundered. "Charnas!'' she called a second time. ''I have come to give you back your death!''

Charnas was silent and motionless within the flames, but thunder rumbled dangerously close, as if the one-armed man had sent a warning not to interfere with his magic.

''Hurry!'' Lucas said, speaking with his mouth close to her ear.

Nodding, Ashley began the last incantation. ''And death and hell were cast into the lake of fire,'' she intoned. ''This is the second death.''

The fire consumed Charnas. His body burned, held upright by some force beyond Ashley's imagining. The fire sent up a barrier of hazy air and blue flames. Within the luminous cone of the flames, Charnas seemed bathed in the beauty he had possessed when he had walked the earth as a living man. Ashley watched and was numbed by his beauty.

Then it was over. Charnas's flesh disappeared. His bones were clothed only in a charred residue. They hung together for a moment, then clattered into the water, separating and washing downstream. The flames seemed to follow his bones, licking them, eating at them. Then even the flames were gone.

Ashley fell to her knees, holding her hand over her mouth, not yet believing what she had seen.

Lucas knelt beside her. ''He's gone,'' he said. ''He's dead.'' His voice seemed full of wonder. He hugged her, then pulled away. ''Look,'' he said, pointing across the stream.

Nikki still lay on the opposite bank, her pale legs bicycling as she screamed her unhappiness.

''Come on,'' Lucas said. ''Let's go get her.''

TWENTY

Three days later, Vernettie entered Ashley's bedroom with a steaming mug in her hand. Ashley dropped the tissue she had been using to wipe her nose. After making it back to the house on the day that Charnas was destroyed, she had fallen ill, but was nearly well now.

She sat up, straightening her gown. Vernettie waited until she had taken the mug, then signaled for her to hold it with both hands. "It's chicken consomme. Rosamar's mother sent it over. It's not as good as mine, but it will do."

Ashley smiled. "Is Rosamar here?" she asked.

"Was," Vernettie answered. "Clay drove her to gymnastics class. He wants to watch."

Ashley shook her head, but didn't comment on the budding relationship between Clay and Rosamar. There was something else on her mind. "What's the new nanny like?" she asked. "I heard Mom let her in a few minutes ago."

"Seems nice enough," Vernettie said with a shrug, "except she's too young."

"Twenty-two," Ashley said. She took a sip of the consomme and then lowered the mug. "Do you mind having someone else take care of Nikki, instead of you?"

Vernettie folded her hands in her lap and looked down at them for a moment, twisting her thin wedding band. "No. Fact is, I've been thinking it's about time to retire altogether. I aim to enjoy myself a little before it's too late."

Ashley looked at Vernettie and noted the glistening of moisture in her eyes, but decided to say nothing. She set the mug down on the bedside table and then climbed out of bed and went over to the window. She looked through the trees toward where the creek wound through the cypresses.

"Charnas is gone," Vernettie said, coming up behind her. "You can stop watching out that window for him." Ashley could feel Vernettie's warm breath on her cheek.

Through the first fevered day after the storm, Ashley had needed to be reassured again and again that Charnas had been destroyed. Even now, she found it hard to believe. She kept switching back and forth between the two images of him that seemed most clear: the beautiful young man lying helplessly ill in a mud-walled room and the terrifying, ruined man who leaned over Nikki's crib. It was still hard for her to reconcile the two images.

"When I'm well, I'm going to make sure. I'm going back to the lair," she said. In the last few days, she had often wondered if Charnas had longed for the peace and oblivion of a true grave. In all of her visions of him as a young man, she had never felt him to be an evil person. He had only been unwilling to accept what must happen. He had bargained for survival for himself and for his lineage, and he had bargained badly.

"There won't be anything to see at the lair,"

185

Vernettie said, putting her thin hand on Ashley's shoulder. "Lucas and Clay have already been there."

Ashley nodded. "I know," she said. "Lucas told me."

"Speaking of Lucas," Vernettie said, squeezing Ashley's shoulder, "he's coming up to see you as soon as he gets through directing the men unloading lumber for the gazebo."

"How are his hands today?" Ashley asked. She felt along the length of a strand of her hair and noted that it needed washing.

"They're coming along fine," Vernettie said. "I've still got him using the salve I made up. You know, he's always asking me questions about how you're doing."

Ashley felt herself blush, but she only said, "I have a lot to thank him for. Clay and Rosamar, too."

Vernettie patted Ashley's shoulder. "For the first time since he was a little boy, Clay's been asking about Grandmother Birdie. He used to be interested, but after he got teased a time or two at school for telling one of the old stories, he turned against Grandmother Birdie's kind of knowledge. I guess I have something to be grateful for, too."

Ashley's thoughts went back to Charnas. "I wonder if Charnas really had all of those powers I thought he might have," she said. "Like controlling the snakes. Reading my mind. I didn't know everything that I should have known about him. I didn't realize who he was until it was almost too late. I kept making mistakes."

"And you'll keep on making them," Vernettie said. "That's part of life. And another part is not always having all the answers. There's some things not even dreamers know."

"Or ought to know," Ashley said, thinking of the secret chants of the one-armed man.

A bell jingled in the nursery. Ashley listened, then turned and crossed her room. She headed for the connecting dressing room.

"Don't you go in that nursery," Vernettie said, following. "You're going to get that baby sick."

"No, I'm not," Ashley said, crossing the connecting rooms. She stopped at the threshold. "I'm not going all the way in."

From where Ashley stood, the yellow crib bumper hid her view of her sister. All she could see was Nikki's feet as they cycled, sometimes accidentally kicking the bell suspended from her mobile. Whenever that happened, Nikki would stop moving for a moment.

Ashley smiled. Soon Nikki would discover the connection between her feet and the ringing bell. She was learning something new every day. She had begun turning herself over from her stomach to her back more often. She was a pretty remarkable little girl to have survived all that she had. And she hadn't even had a sniffle to show for it.

Ashley hadn't heard her mother approaching, but she entered the room from the hallway door, smiling over at Ashley and Vernettie. She crossed to the crib, bending forward to smile down at Nikki and then looking up at Ashley. "I'm bringing her down to meet her nanny," she said.

Drawing in a deep breath, Ashley felt a tug in the region of her heart. Vernettie's hand tightened on her shoulder. Vernettie must be feeling regrets of her own. Together they watched as Ashley's mother carried Nikki out of the room, and then, after a moment,

Vernettie lowered her hand. "I was thinking about growing worms," she said.

"What?" Ashley said, laughing and then regretting the laughter because it brought on a fit of coughing.

Vernettie grasped Ashley's arm above the elbow and propelled her back toward her bedroom. When Vernettie had Ashley situated back in the bed, with the mug of consomme again in her hands, she said, "I've been thinking that I'm not getting any younger. It's time to move on to new adventures."

"Growing worms?"

Vernettie nodded. "There's a little bait shop near where I live. They've already said they'll take all the worms I can sell them. I'm going to be a business-woman."

Ashley shook her head.

"So what about you?" Vernettie asked. "Now that I've convinced your parents that your concussion was responsible for that little fire-setting incident and you don't need counseling after all, are you going to buckle down and become an engineer or a rocket scientist, the way they want you to?"

"No," Ashley said, resting the mug on the coverlet. She met Vernettie's gaze. They both knew that the dreaming would occupy Ashley through much of her life. "It's time for me to find out about my dreams, and not anyone else's. This fall, the school is offering a journalism class and also a senior seminar on myths and traditions." She looked up at Vernettie. "I just wrote a petition asking to be allowed into both classes. I think they'll make a good beginning."